NAKIETA CALHOUN

TO KILL A BROWN BROWN GIRL

WHEN YOU'RE JUST NEVER ENOUGH

Published by Krystal Lee Enterprises (KLE Publishing) Copyright © 2024 by Nakieta Calhoun. All rights reserved. Please send comments and questions:
Krystal Lee Enterprises
770-240-0089 Ext. 1
sales@KLEPub.com

To Reach the Author:
Email: nakieta@klepub.com
Web: NakietaCalhoun.com

ISBN: 978-1-945066-54-2

TABLE OF CONTENTS

PROLOGUE

Over the disco lights and the hit song flashlight by George Clinton and Parliament blasting, Memphis Cox and I still managed to lock eyes. Chocolate men had always been my type, so seeing Memphis was right up my alley. After about an hour, Memphis finally made his move. "What's happening, light skin?"

I admit, his game wasn't all that, but I didn't object. It didn't take long before me and Memphis were spending all our time together. Memphis didn't care that I had four children and stayed with my mom. I felt like my mom just hated–me.

So, having Memphis come into me and the kids' lives was just what we needed. After I revealed the news that I was pregnant with my fifth child, my mom demanded that I get out of her home My sister April, threw my purse behind me.

Me and my kids were homeless, but only until I was able to inform Memphis. This man seemed to be heaven sent and my kids loved him. He got us an apartment, and soon after, he put a ring on it. We had no idea the man we knew was only a representative who would soon stop showing up. Months later, I gave birth to my fifth child. Hmm, "What should we name her?" "Nyla, Nyla Cox."

Prologue

INTRODUCTION

This morning started out like any other typical morning: eyes open, looking up to the ceiling, wondering why must I get up. Why couldn't my mom have given me that light color complexion,that seemed to be so appealing? Rather than me getting my dad's dark Whoopi Goldberg's complexion. I had no doubt that I was beautiful, or was it all in my mind?

Was I only good for fucking? Should dark-skinned women not be trusted? Were we as aggressive and combative as people say?

Those are just some of the thoughts that drove me crazy before I could attempt to thank God for the crummy job he had done with my life. For some reason, my mind was doing a number on me this morning; I was thinking dark. I mean darker than the color of my skin, darker than a black grizzly bear in hibernation dark.

My legs wanted to retreat to the floor; however, my mind said bitch stay put! All I could think to do was empty the bottle of sleeping pills sitting on the nightstand into my stomach. I want to end this shit – right here and now.

How–did I let my mind get the best of me? How did I let it get so bad that I anticipated suicide? Regret kicked in as my eyes started to slowly close; I began to ponder if anyone else would be a better mother to my kids than me. Could anyone else be a better mother to them than me?

Then there was silence, and all thinking had stopped; then there was nothing.

CHAPTER 1

My life began back in Montgomery, AL where some of my earliest memories are of my father emptying a bottle of Thunderbird into his stomach. I sat at his feet until the bottle was emptied. Then, his chin dropped down onto his chest from too much alcohol consumption.

Soon after, would follow screaming and banging on the walls coming from my parent's bedroom; that made me feel helpless, knowing I couldn't make it okay as a child. I just wanted to see them happy, although that was rarely the case. Montgomery taught me early that my race was equivalent to a roach.

Everybody hated us. We hated us. They killed us. We killed us, but no one really cared. It appeared that no one was reluctant to display contemptuous behavior toward African Americans. White Supremacy was very real and whites were determined to maintain their title. Even if it meant killing what was left of the blacks after we killed ourselves.

Behaviors I've witnessed could not have only been taught through generations of hatred. It had to have been the works of the devil himself. Seeing another human being of my race, wiping spit from their body–their face, to be exact, usually was the white man's choice of degradation until they could catch you alone with several other whites to finish the job.

The South was known for its lynching, rapes, beatings, and any other inhumane crimes against blacks. I vividly remember my mom taking on the role of both mom and dad after the divorce. She would now be responsible for five children and herself. I remember being terrified as a kid when my mom walked me and my sibling through the all-white neighborhood across the bridge to get us to school. Who would walk her back, I thought to myself?

My mom was beautiful; for one; she possessed a light skin complexion. Her face was clear of blemishes. She was thin and didn't resemble a woman who had had five children or any for that matter. She wore a short haircut that in my opinion, fit her more than Halle Berry or any other woman from the 80s or 90s going for this look.

"Keep up, Nyla," my mom would yell anytime I got more than two squares behind on the sidewalk. Even though my shoes weren't made for walking, that's what they did a lot of. I would run just enough to catch up, and reply, "I'm coming, I'm coming." Not that I was in any hurry to get to school because I would have to deal with Brandon.

Brandon Williams was a creep in my kindergarten class. He was the kid from the adjacent neighborhood to mine who looked like a normal kid but carried feelings that shouldn't have been known to children of our age. During story time, Brandon was sure to sit behind me on the carpet to rub all over my arms and legs.

No matter where I sat, he always managed to get behind me. "Settle down Nyla," Mrs. Lot, my kindergarten teacher, would say as my efforts to get away from Brandon failed. Just like that, I was stuck. I had no clue why touching me in that way made Brandon happy. All I knew was it felt gross. I kept the behavior to myself because my mom's plate was already overloaded.

Walking through Chisholm, we knew to be prepared after seeing the first black family move into the all-white neighborhood be tormented. Nothing was impossible. Several white families had moved into the home that the black family was living in now. I think I can speak for everybody when I say we'd never think we'd see the day that a black family would be occupying the space.

Nothing about that investment struck me as brave. The black family had to be just downright stupid. To risk their lives and, for what, to be around people who hated their guts and wanted them dead?

Back across the bridge in our neighborhood, we had encountered the occasional racism. However, it was nothing like what was going on in the all-white neighborhood every day. Little did we know, we would experience something far worse than we had imagined.

While walking to school one morning, I could hear my mom's voice begin to crack just as she told me to keep up. As we approached the home that had now been kept by the stupid blacks, as we called them, for making such a dumb decision to live there. As soon as we entered the square on the sidewalk that placed us directly in front of their house, I could see the word nigger written.

The word was all over the little green house in what appeared to be black spray paint. There was also a wooden cross in the front yard that reeked of gasoline. I could still feel the heat coming from it as if the fire had just burned out minutes before.

Walking to school, we saw and experienced some things that kids just should not have had to see. For instance, being shot at and chased by dogs. The dogs seemed to be racist, in my opinion. We saw the Ku Klux Klan (KKK) riding through on horses. Good thing they weren't in the mood for a nigger chase.

Now, seeing the KKK as a kid was very disturbing, but to see dogs that only chased people of color was just crazy. To think dogs could be trained to be racist is terrible. While running, I would manage to get a glimpse of what was going on behind me and realize none of the white kids were being chased. I'm not sure if it was because they lived in the neighborhood or not, but I knew those people hated us and made sure their dogs felt the same way.

I thought to myself, how could someone

hate another human being this much for the color of their skin, being that race isn't optional? To think these people would stoop to the levels of siccing dogs on us, spitting on us, and shooting at us made me wonder. What satisfaction one could really get from that crude behavior?

Experiencing the hate that existed amongst the black community, I must admit, was far more damaging to our race. Light skin was nice. Brown skin was wrong. Brown brown skin was sin and that's what started my slow death.

CHAPTER 2

A couple of years had passed, and now my older brother Tay would take over the responsibility of ensuring we got to school without a scratch. "Okay, big head," he would say after I headed toward the cafeteria for breakfast each morning. Walking toward the lunchline, I realized Cameron was nowhere in sight, and a spark of relief came over me.

Cameron was beautiful. I could tell by the treatment she received–and not just from the students but the teachers as well. Even when Cameron missed lots of days in school, she was always the teacher's pick for line leader or teacher's helper and anything else, which allowed her to be the face of the class; she did that, too.

Cameron was light-skinned, and her hair wasn't very long. She had older sisters who were fashionable, and she often wore their clothes. So, her attire was usually on point. I held my breath all the way to class from the cafeteria, hoping she would not come today. Once I entered the classroom and noticed Cameron was not sitting at her desk, I instantly put my hands together and looked up. "God, please don't let her come today or anymore," for all I cared. Mrs. Bell was our second-grade teacher.

She was taller than most men I knew or had ever seen before. Her neck was very short, which did not match her body type. She wore this curly wig every day and reeked of moth-balls. "Once you hear your name say present," said Mrs. Bell.

Everyone said present except Cameron Moody. "Yes!" I thought to myself. The morning announcements were coming on just as Mrs. Bell wrapped up her roll call, and still no Cam-eron. My heart pounded with every second that passed.

Usually, if a student was not walking in class right after the Pledge of Allegiance, the chances were they'd be absent for the day. My soul smiled with the thought of no Cameron. That made me the cutest girl in the class. At least until she got over her cold or whatever was keeping her home today.

Most of the morning had passed, and we were lining up for bathroom break. Travis and I had been passing notes across the class. I knew if Cameron were here, it would be her getting the notes, but I didn't care.

I'd take Travis's attention however I could get it. Travis usually only paid attention to Cameron, but today, it would be all about me. It was going to be me, who Travis would be chasing around the playground.

Travis was so cute—the cutest guy in the class, to be exact. He had a dark complexion, was tall for his age, and had beautiful eyes and lips. A birthmark right under his left eye which didn't take away from his beauty, not for one second. He was the best-dressed boy in the class and was my whole reason for coming to school each day. This guy was in my dreams at night; and today, he was in my presence, giving me all his attention.

I watched the clock, sort of like how my mom watched the window once my stepdad was over five minutes late coming home. I couldn't help but anticipate the moment, which made me feel like the prettiest girl in the class. "Line up," shouted Mrs. Bell.

My heart immediately started to pound, and my palms began to sweat. Please don't let me have a wet spot on my butt, I thought. I fell number nine in line, which was a great spot to be. The teacher didn't expect any funny business, although this is where it would take place.

I knew Travis would follow behind me, but I still looked over my right shoulder slightly just to be sure. Sure enough, there he was, pushing past Barry, Larry's twin brother. I could overhear Travis and Dominique plotting about what would happen once we got to the playground. I couldn't wait.

My hatred for Cameron was probably more than a child my age should have displayed. Indeed, I wanted her gone. My stepdad's friend had shown me what Brandon was trying to teach me back in kindergarten. About what men liked and how to keep them satisfied.

He often gave me money to keep my mouth shut about the many times he had forced his dick in me. After a while, it didn't hurt anymore, and it just seemed like easy money. He once asked me if I was his bitch. I agreed while jacking his penis right before he entered into my small body.

I closed my eyes and thought of myself being free like Pippi Longstocking. And just like that, the clear fluid would emerge from the hole on his dick as he made a noise just before zipping up his pants. My mom never suspected any wrongdoings by her dear friend, which is why he was able to have me as much as he wanted with no questions asked.

Maybe I was overthinking what a young boy like Travis wanted from me. But I only knew what I had been taught. Allowing Travis to touch me wherever he liked, I would for sure win him over. And at least it wasn't wrinkled, dry hands.

Once Mrs. Bell escorted us across the crosswalk, we took off like a bull that had just seen a red sheet. I knew to go straight for the slide. This meant Travis could continuously chase me down the slide, then up the steps and back down again. When I got to the top of the steps, for some reason, Travis wasn't coming up behind me.

At that moment, my blue bubble gum ball barrette fell from my hair. So, I reached down to retrieve it. As I brought my head up, I could see why the duo wasn't behind me. They had found someone to replace me.

Kimberly was the new me I thought to myself. She was now the second best to Cameron because – her skin was light; even though her hair was short and her top didn't match her shoes--none of that mattered. She was the "it girl," and I was now out. On the way back to class, she even took the ninth place in line, and I just fell in wherever.

Being at the end of the line, you heard and saw lots of evil things that took place due to the teacher being located at the front of the line. While being careful to remain on the second set of tiles, I saw Horace Flint throwing the hall pass up in the air and catching it as it came back down. That kid was the worst in the state. His family was known to sell drugs and have people killed, which scared me half to death. Horace looked me in the face and said, "I guess they still put dark, ugly people in the back."

This would be a comment that would follow me for the rest of my life, being that I did feel ugly. That comment would hit me harder than the doors slamming on my stepfather's 1971 Chevy Nova. That is what speeded up the process of my death just a bit.

25

CHAPTER 3

My last year in elementary school, which should have been my first year in middle school, but due to the unwanted touching I endured from Brandon, I fell silent and was kept back. It didn't seem too bad at the time because — at least I wouldn't have to deal with him anymore. I was a different person now because of Brandon, and I only wished I knew then how to use my words and not have allowed my voice to be stripped from me.

However, I was about to be in middle school soon, which meant independence. From what I've heard from my older siblings, the dances were epic. All the kids that used to give us hell were there, too, without the help of their dogs and parents; payback was a bitch.

While my siblings were busy rioting at

the middle school, giving the white kids a dose of their own medicine, for the too many times they had been called nigger over the years. I was holding it down at the elementary school, taking down the racist bullies, which left me no time to think about Travis' ass. Besides, I had moved on to older, more mature guys.

No longer did I have to worry about my stepfather's so-called friend. I had learned to blackmail him, which meant I could get the money without the unpleasant touching or him getting on top of me. I was now old enough to know better. I was no longer going to allow him to take advantage of me.

If I may say, some back pay was definitely in order for this creep having his way with me. I would say, "A twenty, please, or I'm telling," and just as quick as the fluid used to leave his penis, the twenty left his pocket. Once I saw how easy it was, I started asking for more money. Eventually, he stopped coming around.

I wanted the money, but the way he had made me feel, his not coming around, wasn't the worst thing that could happen. Of course, I was attracted to the guys my age, but at this point, they just irked my nerves. I really hated when they would touch my butt and run, "What are we five? " I thought.

I knew the dangers of dating older guys, like pregnancy and STDs, but hell, my stepdad's friend managed all those years to avoid them. And besides, you could get any of those things from guys my age. I soon learned that the older guys only wanted a younger girl like me because – they felt girls like me could be trained.

The girls they wanted their age were the red girls, but the red girls were looking for older guys who could spend money on them. Little did I know my training would be placed on hold. Not sure if it was the knots that started forming on my chest or the acne taking over my face, but my mom had become on high alert.

My mom sent me over to my Aunt April's house to keep me out of trouble. My uncle Mike was from New Jersey, and he and my Aunt April were close. So, whenever he came into town, he was sure to hang out with her to catch up and laugh about old times.

Mike wanted to go out with the guys and assured my aunt he'd be back in the morning. So he kissed his two boys good night and went for the door, reeking of too much cologne. When it was time for bed, my aunt was so high from the many joints she had smoked that she told us to sleep wherever our heads hit.

Sleeping in the den on the sofa that turned into a bed was the best due to the floor-model tv; we could watch it until we fell asleep. After watching 227 reruns, I had fallen asleep. While sleeping, I would feel my shirt being removed and then my shorts and panties. I had to tell myself that I was not dreaming.

"What do I do?" I was so afraid to open my eyes. Instead, I just held my legs as tightly as I could, hoping that whoever this was would stop. I could hear the whispers and quickly realized it was my two cousins, Uncle Mike's sons.

After they didn't stop, I prayed that they would see that I was awake and not penetrate me and just leave me alone. I was wrong. They never penetrated me, but they continued to suck my little knots and pulled my legs, trying to get them apart.

"You pull that way, and I'll pull this way," only a fool would think I was still sleeping. After the many failed attempts to spread my legs, my cousins finally gave up. They pulled my clothes up, and acted like nothing had ever happened. I would have liked to act surprised, but once before, I had cousins do something somewhat similar, but never to that extent.

My heart was once again crushed. I loved my cousins and never thought they would do something so horrible. Although I never told anyone, I could never look at them the same. My mom had no clue she was barking up the wrong tree. She was concerned about the outside guys when it was indeed the inside ones that had been in total violation of me. This would be yet another trauma in my life that I wouldn't recover from.

I started to question myself: Why didn't I just wake up swinging? But these were my cousins. How much fun would the holidays have been after that? After that night at Aunt April's, I started staying out a little past my curfew. This made my mom send out a one-woman search party, herself. "Nyla," she would yell through the neighborhood once the streetlights came on. So embarrassing I thought while jumping the fence to get back to the house before she did.

The following day was Pizza Friday, and all I could think about was how my mom had been in my business lately for all the wrong reasons. It was pissing me off so much that I knew the next person who looked at me wrong would catch it. Walking home that afternoon, I stayed to myself.

Right after passing the home of the first black family to move into the all-white neighborhood (that house was now abandoned), my feet stopped, and my fists began to ball when I heard it. Did I just hear what I think I heard? The bully, cleft lip, stupid, ignorant bastard White Mike was pushing around the new black kid, and the word nigger was his word of choice for every other insult.

Before I could stop myself like I really would if I could have, I was on top of White Mike with my fists, taking turns with his face. Of course, my anger was fueled by the night before and I didn't care; Mike had it coming. Once I was done with his ass, I told him, "I better never hear nigger, or any N-word leave your slit lip, nose, or however the words got out of your face ever again."

When I calmed down and was able to think straight, I realized how aggressive and combative I had been. Not that I was ashamed, but it did make me think. Was I the reason for dark women being treated this way? Could I be partly the reason for dark women's reputation? At that moment, I felt like I might faint and had to sit down on the bridge and watch the cars pass as I felt my life slipping away.

CHAPTER 4

Middle school was as lit as my siblings had said. The Homecoming dance was in two weeks and it was the talk of the school. Sure, I tried to get some of the quiet kids to write my name in for homecoming court. But the light-skinned project chicks took all three spots, not that I stood a chance anyway.

I'm sure had I won any spot, the school would have demanded a recount. The school made it no secret who had won homecoming court even before the announcement. "Can't wait to see their dresses," I jokingly said to myself, with them being from the projects and all. Perhaps I was hating. I didn't care; I hated them just as much or even more than they hated me.

Homecoming night was here, and although I had moved on to older, mature guys, there was this one tall, handsome, brown-skinned, well-dressed and charming guy from the neighborhood who everyone wanted. For some reason, he wanted me.

My skin complexion wasn't always a deal breaker, but you can bet the cute guys wouldn't be caught dead with a chick as dark as me. We were only good for one thing, so I had heard. I hadn't had any sexual intercourse as of yet–at least that I had wanted. So technically, that before didn't count. I knew if the school dances were anything like the house parties I'd been to, I would be leaving with wet panties.

Kilo Ali was blasting when my mom pulled around to the gym where the homecoming dance was being held. It seemed like I was out before she could stop the car, and there he was, Keith (that tall, brown-skinned handsome guy who wanted my black ass for some reason) standing outside the gym, waiting for me. Before we could make it to the dance floor, he pulled me close with his hands on my thighs, and I could feel his dick pressed up against my butt.

It didn't feel the same as dancing with other guys. It felt as though he was missing something because – it didn't hang. It just poked me, and for a minute I felt overwhelmed.
36

I knew had I stopped him, I would probably go from a nobody to an ant. Taking this route, at least I could remain a body. We danced all the way up until they were ready to announce homecoming court. This was my cue to politely dismiss myself to the restroom and hope he didn't follow me. Besides, I knew I didn't want to hear that shit anyway.

Instead of going to the restroom, I went straight to the nearest phone and told my mom she could come to get me. I am not sure why dancing with this guy made me so uncomfortable. Maybe it was the feeling of something there, but nothing there; I wasn't sure, but I wasn't sticking around to find out. The next day I tried to avoid him, not that he cared any, because it didn't take long before he was talking to someone else.

I should have known better than to think anyone would want me other than him. I was surprised he did. It was one thing for him to want me, but to be seen with me, oh, I had really messed up. A couple of days passed, and I found an opportunity to say something to Keith. He disrespectfully dismissed me and went on talking to the girl on the bus.

My heart stopped for a second, but I

knew I couldn't look weak. So, I acted like it didn't bother me when I actually wanted to cry. For some reason, Keith got off the bus at my stop, and I was sure he was going to try hugging me but instead; he went into Lisa Richards' house this time. I could swear my heart would stop for good.

Lisa Richards was tall and dark. She often dressed like a boy, and her lips were extremely big. She wore a fan ponytail that just didn't fan out, and in my opinion, she was nowhere near as cute as me. Although we had differences, our double dose of dark skin would land us both in last place anyhow.

I stayed inside for days, missing the bus as much as possible, devastated over the thought of Keith with Lisa. On day three, as my mom shook me awake at 5:00am she said, "You miss that bus today, I'm beating you." At the bus stop, I was being looked at like Casper, the friendly ghost due to my disappearance. I just kept my head down, and my hood pulled tight. I tried to be the first one on the bus so I wouldn't have to make eye contact with anyone, especially Keith.

Not sure where I would sit once I was on the bus though. I couldn't just sit where I usually sat, which was in the back. This area was reserved for the popular kids and those pretending to be. That's for sure where Keith would be seated, so that wasn't an option.

That afternoon Keith got off at my stop again, only this time he yelled, "Wait up." I knew he wasn't talking to me. Then I could hear his footsteps getting closer, "Big head," he repeated twice. Once I realized he was talking to me, I slowed down to give him a chance to catch up.

He talked the whole way to my house, and the only words I could manage to say were, "So now you're screwing, Lisa?" "No, I went over there for her brother." I was able to spot a liar, and he was obviously lying. I decided at that moment what was more important, and that was to play along with his lie and be diminished to a woman who would allow anything from a man just to be considered a woman. I tried as hard as I could not to give in to the many requests from Keith for sex, but I knew he wouldn't wait too long.

Keith had called me up one night, almost demanding that I have sex with him or else, and I did just that. Keith would meet me at the stop sign, and we would walk to his aunt's house from there. The same place where I had assumed so many females had lost their virginity.

He cracked jokes the whole way, so excited for what was about to happen. Not that I was so pretty, but how I was allegedly the last virgin left in the neighborhood. After he was able to add me to his list, he would be the man.

Once we got to his house, he didn't waste any time. We didn't stop in the front room but went straight to his bedroom. When we entered his room, he quickly pulled down my corduroy pants. So many thoughts were going through my head, but I knew not to object.

When my pants hit the floor, he aggressively pushed me back on the bed and pulled my legs apart. I had enough sense to stop him and ask him to put on a condom. He grabbed one from the nearby nightstand and then pushed his penis as deep into my vagina as it would go.

I remembered not really feeling anything, but tears rolling down my face; in the dark room Keith had no clue that I was crying in silence. I hated that I had knowledge of my appearance. At that moment, I wished my father had made me feel pretty. Maybe I wouldn't have allowed a sixteen-year-old boy to manipulate me out of my panties.

Chapter 4

When Keith was done, I wiped my face, pulled my clothes up from my ankles and moved toward the door. Keith didn't say anything. I imagined that it was because he was knowledgeable of what a virgin should feel like, and he could tell I was not one. He walked me back to the stop sign, and just like that, that was that.

Rumors were already going around the next day about me and Keith. I was trying my best to deny them, but there was more to Keith than what I had known. Keith had also taken the virginity of Lisa, Tina, and Terry, who were sisters, if I may add. Rumors were going around that Kim was pregnant by him.

I could only wonder why no one warned me about this guy. Then I thought to myself, they were probably thinking the same thing. As I struggled to make sense of it all, I came across something rather disturbing. All of us were dark-skinned except Kim. We probably all had low self-esteem. Kim was probably pregnant due to her light skin complexion, which I'm sure gave Keith comfort knowing chances were their child would be light too.

Due to our need for acceptance we made ourselves easy prey to a guy like Keith. That just made me sick to my stomach so much. I couldn't eat or sleep for days and I just knew I would die.

CHAPTER 5

After dating that creep Keith, I must admit I was a bit vulnerable; since my cover was already blown. I jumped on the first guy to call me cute, which I had strong doubts about. That guy was Lorenzo Carter, low haircut, chunky, not very tall, dark skin, drop-out, and had nothing going for himself.

I was only fourteen, and Lorenzo was twenty-one, living with his Aunt. She could care less about him fucking my brains out in the other room as long as we were not too loud for her to hear All My Children and General Hospital. His Aunt usually just knocked on the wall as a warning, indicating we were too loud. This point of my life is what I called the point of no return because – my first sexual experience was involuntary, and now, I was just out of control. It was no secret, so any goody two shoes left in me had left right along with my goodies.

Sex with Lorenzo was definitely different from my other two encounters. It reminded me of what my mom had been telling me, which was to stay my ass in a child's place. It wasn't that Lorenzo's penis was ridiculously big or anything. It was more so him wanting to do things that I had heard people say to one another as insults.

I had never had oral sex performed on me before, and I most definitely had never given it. So when Lorenzo went past my belly button, I was shocked and honestly was unsure what was the purpose of this. Lorenzo kind of played around down there, and then I guess he decided to take it up a notch.

Lorenzo pulled back my pussy lips, exposing my clitoris, and began moving his tongue extremely fast. His tongue continued moving, releasing saliva onto me as my body tensed up, my toes curled, and my eyes were wide and rolled back into my head. A wave of heat came over me as my hands began to sweat. I was losing control and didn't realize that my moans had turned into screams.

I momentarily wondered, was I having a seizure due to the disfiguring of my body, although the shit felt too good. I clearly wasn't in need of medical attention. Just as Lorenzo's Aunt's knocks turned into beating, my body began shaking, and my hips were rolling. All I could do was grab his head closer until whatever was happening to me was over.

After what seemed to be the best feeling I had ever felt, I released Lorenzo's head. Still breathing hard and biting my bottom lip, I was allowing my vagina time to return back to its original form. Because at that moment, it felt like a blood pressure cuff that had expanded. I analyzed that this must have been what a person felt the first time they got high and continued chasing that feeling; although it probably was never the same.

Oral sex felt good, but I must admit, I never saw the moon and the stars again. My mom started working at night, and would sleep most of the day, which gave her darling Nyla all the room to play. So that high alert she once had for me was no more. Some nights, I would spend the night at Lorenzo's and as long as I beat my mom home, all was good.

One night, my mom caught me red-handed. She came home early, and as I walked in the door, she was sitting right there waiting for my pitiful arrival. My mom would appear sad but angry. Her hair was a mess, I assumed, from holding the top of her head, anticipating the dreadful discovery of where I could have been so late. I'm sure my mom had almost walked the tiles off the floor, and at this point, she was just worn out and wanted to face me.

"Where have you been?" My mouth hung open, but nothing was coming out. "Where have you been?" My mom screamed louder this time. Words never left my mouth. She left the room. I stood by the door for hours just in case I needed to run. She never came back and never spoke of it again.

In my head, I had messed up with the only light-complexioned person who had loved or even liked me, so I wasn't cleaning up my act now. This would have been the perfect opportunity for my mom to put me on birth control, but I think she was tired and had given up on me. And how could I blame her? My mom had just witnessed what she thought was her innocent and sweet daughter turn into a slut right before her eyes.

Things had gotten weird after that night between me and my mom, not that I really cared. I didn't really see her that much now anyway, so I would continue my downhill spiral. Lorenzo's Aunt fed him like a garbage disposal. No wonder why he was so big. His Aunt brought him two Monster burgers, two Star burgers, a double cheeseburger, large fries, and a large vanilla milkshake from the burger joint up the street.

I had stopped eating there after they discontinued the fried chicken, but this particular day that Star burger was screaming, come-into-the-light. I had eaten the star burger like I hadn't eaten one in years. That made me think to myself, could I be pregnant?

I mean, I hadn't seen my period last month, but I didn't think I could possibly be pregnant. Not sure why I thought procrastination was a good idea, like it would make my problem go away. I let another month go by. Out of the blue (one day, after sex), Lorenzo said, turn around.

"What?"" Once I turned around, Lorenzo grabbed his mouth; his eyes were wide, and then he dropped his hand, "You pregnant." Tears instantly started uncontrollably rolling down my face. Lorenzo was much more experienced than I was, and for some dumb reason, I would have made an ass out of myself, assuming he was taking the necessary precautions not to get me pregnant.

Of course, Lorenzo and I were having un-protected sex almost every day. I never thought about the consequences of my actions until the time came. After Lorenzo made the statement about me possibly being pregnant, we didn't talk too much about it because – I still was sure to beat my mom home even though I had been caught once.

So, I needed to get dressed, "I'll call you later," Lorenzo said pitifully as I walked through the door. A couple of weeks passed, and my mom wanted to visit my older sister, Kizzy in North Carolina. I packed my bags, kicking and screaming, because – I did not want to go. But no way was my mom leaving me behind.

My mom couldn't figure out for the life of her why I was so uncomfortable on the Grey-hound and I definitely wasn't ready to tell her why. We finally made it to my sister's house after six hours. All I wanted to know was where we would be sleeping. I was exhausted.

I guess word had gotten around the neighborhood because – my sister Quay back home called my mom early the next morning to tell her the horrible news. My sister had always resented me due to Lorenzo. She would tell anyone who would listen that Lorenzo was hers first with no regard for how much of a slut that made me look like. Although I had no clue if it was true, Lorenzo sure never spoke of it, but at that moment, I sure wished she was still with his ass and not me.

I was out back, and my mom busted through the screen door, "Nyla, I know like hell you ain't pregnant!" My mouth hung open much like the last time she caught me in an enormous lie when no words came out. My mom had told me whatever I did in the dark would come to the light. Sure enough, the spring-covered trees were turning into the fall-naked trees, and everything was becoming visible.

I knew I had really done it this time. My mom was so disappointed that she cried harder than I had ever seen before, and it was all my fault. I knew I had messed up when I missed my period but when I saw those tears falling from my mom's eyes. I had to be face to face with the damage I had caused and at that moment, I would have done anything to take her pain away.

That night, my mom caught me sneaking in I guess I had made myself believe she no longer cared; apparently, she did. The newfound knowledge would be the first time I thought to myself that just killing myself would be easier.

CHAPTER

On the trip back, my mom looked out the window and didn't say one word the whole ride. I had never seen her like that. I felt it would be best to just keep quiet as well. Once we made it back to sweet home Alabama, which no longer seemed sweet, the house was quiet.

I walked to the room with my head facing the floor in its rightful place to express my shame, disappointment, and failure. Over my fifteen years, I had enough to deal with when it came down to the color of my skin. Now, I had one more reason to be frowned upon.

Upon my return, I just knew Lorenzo would be blowing the phone up. But I hadn't heard from him, and I had been back almost a week. Everyone was talking about the 1992

Chevrolet Caprice Lorenzo's mom had just gotten him. They were very popular cars in Montgomery, and they were, quote-unquote, a dope boy's car.

He was passing by every hour on the hour as I stood on the porch, but never did he say anything. I knew if my mom saw me, it would only make matters worse. I did all I could to try and make up for the mess I had made by doing chores around the house. One day, while taking the trash out, I saw Lorenzo's car parked across the street.

A light complexion girl with curly hair who appeared to be mixed was visiting; there was no way she would be interested in Lorenzo. There had to be another reason for his car being parked directly in front of her house. Was this the reason for his numerous drive-bys? I decided to stay outside just to see if they would come out together. After an hour, my pregnant bladder was stressing that it needed to be emptied. I ran in to relieve myself.

I was back out in what seemed like under a minute. I made it back to the porch just in time to see his car pulling off, which gave me the impression he had been watching and waiting for me to go inside so that I wouldn't have enough evidence. Then, he could still look me in the face and lie because – what I didn't see wasn't tea; it was pure speculation. That was all Lorenzo needed, a speck of reasonable doubt to lie.

I had no clue who was inside of the car. Lorenzo made sure of that by hitting the accelerator in a way that insisted he was in a hurry. Later that night, while my mom was at work, I waited everyone else out and quietly went through the back door. "Please don't let my mom come home early tonight," I said as I walked to Lorenzo's house in full fight gear, like I wasn't four months pregnant.

As I got closer, I could see his car was parked out front. I walked to the back of the house to knock on the window. Through the torn blinds, I could clearly see the light skin of the female, her breast spread apart as she laid back on the bed, drooling as if she was over-worked. Judging from the overgrowth of hair on her vagina, she thought her looks were good enough to make one overlook the dying mainte-nance that her vagina was due for. I could spot Lorenzo's horribly shaped body anywhere as they both lay there asleep.

I began to beat on the window as if I

wanted to break it, and they both began pulling up the covers to seek cover like I hadn't already seen enough to know the truth. I could hear the curiosity in the female's voice as she asked over and over, "Who is that?" I knocked louder and louder and screamed insults, but he never came to the door.

I knew it would be bad if my mom came home, so I made the decision to leave as my anger turned into tears. I cried all the way home. My brother was up watching tv, and I just walked past him like he wasn't even there, got into bed, and continued to cry myself to sleep.

The next morning, I woke up to my mom throwing my things in garbage bags. I guess my brother had ratted me out. "I want you out!" I cried and pleaded with her, " I don't have any-where to go."

"You should have thought about that before you decided to be grown." Looking at my brother as I walked past him with my book bag, not knowing where I would go, I knew he felt bad for telling; he didn't know it would go this far. Even after last night, I still had no other option but to go to Lorenzo's.

As I got closer, I could see his car wasn't

there. I knocked on the door anyway, and no one answered. At that moment, reality started to set in, I was all alone and pregnant. After about an hour of me sitting there, Lorenzo and his Aunt pulled up with grocery bags; it appeared they had been to the store.

Lorenzo and his aunt walked into the house, and I followed behind them. He didn't mention the night before, and neither did I. He explained to his Aunt that my mom had put me out, and I had nowhere to go. I listened to her fuss for a while, but it was over quickly, and she commuted to her room with a bottle of vodka in one hand and a chicken leg in the other.

Later that night, Lorenzo would climb on me three times like he wasn't just in the same bed with another chick. I knew this had to be what a prostitute felt like. I didn't want him on me, but I had no other choice. Laying there in silence as he humped on me as if there wasn't a baby growing directly under him. At this point, I was just working my nerves up to take my mom, Lorenzo, myself, and even this unborn baby out of misery by slitting my wrist, allowing the blood to leave my useless body.

CHAPTER 7

Thank God it didn't take long before my mom let me back in the house. Although it was like living in hell because – no one spoke a word to me (it was like I wasn't even there). Unable to go back to school, I felt that my life was over. I would be a fifteen-year-old mom with a seventh-grade education.

To top it all my skin was darker than the night I had walked in to get myself in this predicament, so surely my appearance wasn't going to be of any help. My mom continued to express how she didn't give a damn about me going to school to anyone that asked. She would say, "Had I not been grown and gotten pregnant I could have been in school."

I continued to be a waste of space, only

leaving to go to doctors' visits and afterward re-
turning to my uncomfortable daybed that slept
like a couch. While my mom got my bitter sister,
Quay, a brand-new queen-sized bed to punish
me. For the next five months, I remained quiet
and tried my best to stay out of the way, even
though an actual human was growing inside of
me.

Early one morning, I felt wet, and I was
not sure what I was experiencing. I went to the
restroom. I didn't feel the need to pee, but fluid
was rushing down my legs. My mom would be
leaving for work in an hour, so I stayed quiet
even after the pains started coming back-to-
back. I still felt it would be better to let her walk
out rather than me knocking on her door for
help. Once my mom came out of her room, I
still was nervous to inform her of what was going on.

I mean she hadn't spoken to me in so
long that I still wasn't sure if she would entertain
my needs. "Mom," I said, "I think I'm in labor."
She walked into the room. I had no idea what
she would say or do, but it just so happened to
be the first time in almost a year that she had
spoken to me and shown any form of support.

My mom let me know the importance of

her going to work and instructed me to tell my stepfather if the pain got too bad so he could get me to the hospital. She assured me she would meet me there later. Little did she know, the pain was already too bad; before my mom could leave the neighborhood, I was knocking on the door asking my stepfather to please take me to the hospital because I was in labor.

I had never cramped badly, so the pain I was feeling was unbearable, and there was no feeling that could compare to the stabbing pain that was shooting through me every two minutes. It felt as though the pain would never stop. Once we pulled up to the emergency room entrance, my mind told me to jump out, but my body said differently.

Eventually, my mind and body were on the same page. I slowly got out of the car, holding my lower stomach as if my baby would hit the pavement if I didn't offer the security. Anxiety started to set in while I was being wheelchaired down the hall by a nurse who was no doubt judging me with every turn of the wheel.

"Undress and put on the gown with the opening to the back," the nurse repeated this twice as if, due to my age, I was too ignorant to understand. I wasn't sure who told Lorenzo I was in labor. He and my mom walked into the room minutes apart as though one fell back with the intention of allowing the other to enter before so they could avoid close contact with each other.

The sound of the baby monitor was the only noise circulating in the room. If not for my baby's heartbeat, a pin hitting the floor could be heard. After receiving an epidural, the time passed fairly fast. Before I knew it, my legs were being spread, my feet were being placed in metal holders, my mom on the right and Lorenzo on the left side, and the doctor looked me in the eyes and said, "push."

A total of five pushes and Emerald was here, seven pounds sixteen ounces. I was thankful that her skin was light like my mom's and not dark like mine. I took one look at her while she cried to the top of her lungs. I thought to myself, I have nothing to offer this child. I was nothing more than a statistic who would be proud of me being their mom. My mom was young enough to raise her. Maybe I'll just send Lorenzo out for pain meds and take them all during the night.

Emerald was perfect; her skin was light, her hair was full and lying flat on her head. She even had a beauty mark; a mark that most women had to fake by having it tattooed on their faces. She honestly did not resemble Lorenzo or me, although she did have his big forehead. Mentally, I wasn't ready to take my baby girl home, but I didn't have much of a choice. I had already surpassed my two-day stay at the hospital, so it was time to be discharged.

There wasn't a welcome home party or anything of that nature when we arrived home, but the energy was different. And for the first time in almost a year, everyone was talking to me again and not giving me dirty looks. In my head, I thought it was fake. But I was too excited to exist again–the feeling of being a part of a family again meant the world to me.

I wasn't going to mess that up. So, being rude was the last thing on my agenda and it was all thanks to Emerald. At night, I would dream of my mom and siblings speaking to me again, but I was not sure what my family wanted to prove by not speaking to me before.

There were many days that I couldn't get the knife to cut deep enough into my wrist to kill myself or even get lightheaded, for that matter. I wondered if my family would have been so quick to change their minds if my baby had come out dark like me with nappy hair or no hair. Would my family have started back talking to me again?

I treaded lightly in that house. I knew if my family was okay with not speaking to me for this long, what else were they capable of? What extreme would they really go to to prove a point?

My chest began pounding, and my breaths felt short. I knew I needed to take my baby and head for the daybed. I wanted out, but not like this. I was sure my death would be the work of me, not health-related, and by the desperate measures this family took to make me feel like shit. I knew it would not be long before I could indeed get the knife to go deep enough.

CHAPTER
8

Lorenzo couldn't keep a job, and I had just gotten my first job at a fast food restaurant. When asked what position I was interested in, I couldn't even spell cashier. Life was going to be extremely hard I thought to myself. "Bro, howyou spell cashier?"

It was a good thing he had come inside and didn't drop me off. I felt so dumb, but at least I could buy pampers and provide for my baby. My dad stepped up and helped a lot where he could. It really surprised me because – I hadn't seen a lot of him since the divorce; my mom had checked out. I needed him to check in even though I understood how she felt.

My dad would give anybody a chance, being that he was no angel himself. He didn't hate Lorenzo; he only wished that he could keep a job. But that wasn't even a reason my dad could judge, being that he had his fair share of shortcomings when it came down to jobs.

My father never expressed disappointment in me becoming a mother at the young age of fifteen. He honestly never spoke about it. I assumed my father was consumed with grief, being that – he wasn't there to teach me how a man should treat me, so he kept any opinions to himself.

Lorenzo had the perfect job right behind the neighborhood. In fact, he could walk through the woods to work until the boss man got tired of his tardiness, absences, and extra-long breaks. He eventually fired him, and Lorenzo moved on to a grocery store. Stocker was the position Lorenzo would hold at the store, which was perfect, being that – Emerald's WIC always ran short. Lorenzo had no problem sticking a can of milk in his pants.

Lorenzo's position was overnight, so he always stopped by to visit Emerald in the mornings before going home. I attempted to attend a credit school once. But Lorenzo's Aunt quickly opposed the action, after about a month of Emerald having to stay all day.

Lorenzo got fired from the store after about six months but he and his Aunt still weren't willing to have Emerald all day, even if it was my only way to have a future. Lorenzo would come up with a brilliant plan, at least he thought it would be. His plan was to rob a guy he had been watching for days.

What Lorenzo failed to record was the other gentleman that stayed in the home, and only left at night to go to work. Lorenzo would return to the home as planned the next morning after his week-long stakeout to move forward with the robbery. Only, he was greeted by an individual at the end of the hall who was disturbed by his kicks to the door in an attempt to kick the door down.

The man fired off one shot at Lorenzo, and the bullet went past him like he was Keanu Reeves from the movie "The Matrix," as Lorenzo's body bent backward to avoid being shot. This gave him an opportunity to run like hell. He made it to the car and jumped in with the man still running behind him!

The man would fire again, this time shattering the back window and another shot that penetrated the brake light. Lorenzo sped off and returned home, with everyone pointing and talking as he passed through the neighborhood. They all tried to speculate what could have happened to the car that once turned heads for its popularity and is now turning heads for its unpleasantness.

Lorenzo went straight for the phone, called his mom, who stayed in Nashville, and informed her of what had just taken place. He needed out of Montgomery much like Will Smith needed to leave from Philadelphia in the Fresh Prince of Bel- Air, he needed out fast. His mom wouldn't be able to get there until the weekend, but being–that he was raised by his Aunt, of course, he didn't expect his mom to stop what she was doing even if it did mean life or death.

Lorenzo covered the car with as many sheets as he could and bricks to hold the sheets down. Then, he called me to deliver the news that he would be leaving. "Leaving? What do you expect me and the baby to do?" "I'll try and send for you, but for now, I gotta lay low." When he dropped the phone, I immediately went into tears.

I didn't make enough for daycare. My mom was only providing me with shelter, and my dad was MIA again. What was I going to do? This would be Lorenzo's first step toward death but would be another step closer for me into my venture. Soon, I would work up enough nerve to follow through on those thoughts of my early demise.

CHAPTER 9

Lorenzo made it to Nashvillie safely, and of course, he kept his promise. Not to send for me–but the one when he said he needed to lay low. He continued to do just that even after his arrival. Months had passed, and the last time I spoke to Lorenzo was the day of his arrival in Nashville because he had been ghosting me ever since.

Tax time was approaching, and I had no intentions of raising this child alone; even if it meant Lorenzo would just be a babysitter. It would be more than I had as of now. Besides, I had heard great things about this city and wanted to experience it for myself. I knew I would need a couple of things if I wanted to be successful in Nashville. Even though I hadn't been given an official invitation, I was still getting out of this situation at my mom's.

Lorenzo knew I would be getting a healthy size check this year, being that I had a child to claim. Sure enough, he was resurrected, calling right on schedule, talking bout' he had been tied up looking for work. Lorenzo had no real explanation as to why he hadn't spoken to me or to his baby in months. Of course, I was angry, but that was nothing new.

After what appeared to be no effort at all on Lorenzo's part, I suggested that I should move to Nashville for a fresh start. I would provide us with the only source of income. Although my mom had shown little interest in me the last two years, she gave me hell on my way out of the house. She knew my leaving would be a bad idea, but I had to find out on my own.

Lorenzo met Emerald and me at the bus station, smiling ear to ear, which, in my opinion, was more about the funds that were attached to us, not the baby and me. We headed straight to Lorenzo's mom's house from the bus station, and his phone was on emergency mode. It was ringing and vibrating the whole ride, which would explain why we hadn't heard from him in months. Once we arrived at Lorenzo's parent's house, his mom would perform as though she was happy to see the baby and me.

But I knew deep down that she really hated my guts. Lorenzo's mom wasn't concerned with me taking her son. She just hated any woman who could take away from her being the most important woman in the room and forbid it being a dark one like myself.

Lorenzo took his phone outside due to its unwillingness to cooperate and there he would remain on the phone for hours. Why am I putting up with this I thought. "You ready to go?" Lorenzo asked me when he entered the house after his phone sex or whatever was taking place in the driveway.

"Where are we going this late?" Lorenzo's parents weren't going to dare get in trouble, so – they made it clear that due to me being a minor still in the eyes of the law, we would need to stay in a motel. In my mind, I didn't want to sleep with Lorenzo. I just wanted to sleep, but being that I was all too familiar with Lorenzo, I knew if he didn't want to fuck my vagina raw, it would have been weird.

We ended up in some sleazy motel in the Clarksville area for the night while Emerald stayed back with his family. This is where my nice size tax check began to turn into fun size, although the fun wasn't included. I allowed Lorenzo to give the impression that he had not had sex since the last time he had seen me.

He licked every part of my body, and I do mean every. I didn't decline because all I could think of was him passed out–sleep, so I could go through his phone. Before the saliva could depart his lips good, I was inside his phone wondering who Jane Doe was. I was sure she had to be a light-skinned hoe due to his history.

Entering Lorenzo's phone, I wasn't prepared for what I had seen. The hoe's skin was lighter than light; the bitch was white. At that moment, I paused to think of how pleased Lorenzo's mom would be with his choice of a woman.

Lorenzo's mom was the typical definition of a disaster. She had been a teen mom and a dropout, and to top it all off, she was a darker-skinned black woman. She was no victim of statutory rape, but maybe that of a generational curse. Leaving Lorenzo behind with her aunt helped her advance in life.

An extra dose of curses would also help Lorenzo's mom manage to land a spot in the corporate world. There she experienced first-hand which skin shades were marketable. She had no intention on her family continuing down the unmarketable path.

My soul had never screamed before but on this particular night, it was on a roller coaster. I wasn't waiting till morning to address this shit. I woke Lorenzo with a slap to his face, and a Mortal Kombat combination followed, "What the hell?" I just continued swinging, asking him to hit me back.

I assumed that's the message I sent because he knocked my ass to the floor. Once on the floor, I thought to myself, what have I gotten myself into? I couldn't go back home due to the terrible fight between my mom and me about moving to Nashville. Knowing that if we got kicked out of the room, it wouldn't be anywhere else to go this late. I took a seat on the stained mahogany chair and tried to pull myself together.

Surely this wasn't the only thing Lorenzo had done to me, and I'm sure it wasn't going to be the last. Just the thought of dealing with this bastard for one more second made me nauseous. My breathing became very heavy, and I blanked out.

CHAPTER 10

Once I came to, I wasn't the happiest, but while out, I did dream of me and Emerald peacefully living without Lorenzo's cheating ass. I was determined to make my dream a reality. I hit every restaurant and apartment complex the next day on the bus. "I'm not wasting a penny on his trifling ass this year," I said to myself as I waited for the manager at the restaurant to call my name for an interview.

Flipping burgers sure wasn't going to get me and Emerald any closer to that dream. I was determined to start somewhere, even if it meant I would be the only black in the building. It would take me changing buses twice and a train to get to work in the mornings. It took me two hours and an additional two hours to get back.

Meanwhile, Lorenzo was still having

problems finding a job. On my first day on the job, I was already exhausted from traveling but I worked hard to fit in and not stick out. Although my color would make things very hard in that area. Rico was the restaurant manager, and he would make it his business to make sure I was treated like a pariah.

On top of his joking about my extremely dark skin, he made sure to always have that one last thing for me to do so I would miss my bus. That added fifteen minutes to my two hours and guaranteed my walk home would be in the dark. It wouldn't take long before the other Hispanics joined in on the humiliate Nyla train, and I was over it.

On top of the four hours, I would miss Emerald every day; I was done. I knew the next day Rico would be putting me in the back window to collect money. So I patiently waited for the cars to wrap around the building. Then I said, "I quit."

I threw my sweaty uniform shirt right in Rico's face just in time to catch the next bus passing. My mom had always told us never quit a job without a back-up but my days of being a victim of racism were over. Although my days of not listening to my mom should have been overdue.

Not sure what the next move was going to be. I headed out the next morning as if I was heading to work even though I was unemployed. I never tried to report the manager and his staff for the many inappropriate comments because – where I was from, it was normal to be black and not favored. I guess, in so many ways, it was normal to me.

This time, I searched for work close and found employment the same day. Why couldn't Lorenzo do the same? I thanked the manager for the opportunity and ran to catch the bus. Arriving home while it was still light out meant I would be able to do more with Emerald, which made me happy.

I had started to settle into my new life. I had friends and was even able to purchase a car with my return that next year. Sure enough, it only rained outside when I didn't have my umbrella. I started feeling sick; surely I couldn't be pregnant again. Me and Lorenzo had sex maybe once a week, if that, and even then, I made it my business to play–sleep in hopes of him just going away.

The pregnancy test would prove me wrong in a matter of seconds. Two lines would pop up and my head would drop down. "What am I going to do?" I will figure things out. What Lorenzo thought he had figured out would land us in even more trouble. Me being barely able to get out of bed in the morning gave Lorenzo more time to run the streets, and that would be something that I would regret.

Lorenzo and I were able to get a new place. Having our place made us a little happier, which made Emerald happy. I was able to get Lorenzo a job with me. We were finally able to keep up: "No more running an extension cord through the neighbor's window for electricity."

Things had gotten so bad in our last apartment that Lorenzo's parents wanted no part of us, the dusty trio. They would occasionally get Emerald but made it clear they were doing me a favor and not Lorenzo. That was enough reason for Lorenzo's mom to add interest and demand food stamps from me.

It felt good for once to be on track be-cause — I was able to get Emerald into daycare and she loved it. The teachers all loved her. They would always comment on how smart and pret-ty she was. She just took it all in, smiling ear to ear.

Me and Lorenzo usually left for work and came home together every day. Being that I had got him the job I could negotiate his schedule. Life was good, but of course, a rainy day would be coming whenever I left the umbrella at the house. Lorenzo and I had had a wonderful day at work. We laughed all the way home and joked about a customer who literally refused to pay for her fries because they were too hot.

"These hot ass fries burned my lip." The cashier politely asked her, "Did you blow the fry before putting it in your mouth?" We laughed till we cried as if it was happening all over again.

Once we got home, I was exhausted from being pregnant, and my feet felt like I had stood on bricks all day long. Emerald had spent the night with Lorenzo's parents. Instead of them compensating me for the over usage of my food stamp card, they agreed to let her stay the weekend. We had the house to ourselves, at least for the next day or so.

Lorenzo had been complaining of his stomach boiling, so he went straight to the toilet with one hand on his stomach and the other holding his butt. Before I could make it to the top of the stairs, there was a loud pounding noise at the door. "Who is it?" I said with fear in my voice due to the aggression of the person on the other side.

Davidson County Police, my first thought was who was playing until I looked through the peephole and saw actual officers standing on the other side. Once I opened the door, I wasn't sure what was going on. I knew they had the wrong apartment until they spoke Lorenzo's name followed by a warrant for his arrest. I grabbed the lower part of my stomach and my legs became weak.

The officers could care less. They made their way in as Lorenzo was still on the toilet, sweating from a coffee and orange juice mixture from that morning. Not sure if they had been watching through the windows, they went right to the bathroom, opened the door, and demanded that he wipe and come with them.

Once they read him his Miranda Rights and escorted him to the car, I noticed in the other car they had his friend from the old apartment complex who he would run the streets with. When they pulled off, I felt sick. My stomach was in knots, and baby Lorenzo must have felt something wasn't right because -- he wouldn't stop moving. I was all alone with one child and one on the way.

I fell to the floor crying in disbelief, thinking, "Is this what it felt like before I died." I had cried for hours. Nothing changed. My eyes were blood red, and my head was hurting like I had been hit from behind. I couldn't take the stress anymore. My mind led me to the medicine cabinet.

I grabbed the only medicine available to either remove the pain or remove me eternally at that moment. In my head it seemed like the cure for the pain I felt. I began putting the medicine into my body.

CHAPTER 11

After all the medicine, it seemed that God still wouldn't release me from my misery. My eyes opened to look up at the ceiling just as tears began to fall from my eyes. I thought of Baby Lorenzo and hoped that I hadn't hurt him while trying to end my hurt.

Two weeks later, I gave birth to a healthy nine-pound baby boy with Lorenzo's hairline on a cold hospital table all alone. I went back to work in four weeks instead of six. Every Sunday we visited Lorenzo in jail even though we knew the awful amount of time he was facing.

Lorenzo would later be found guilty of robbery and sentenced to five years, leaving me and his two children to pick up the pieces. The kids and I would end up back in Montgomery

AL, where I would meet Steve Cook. Steve was handsome; most times, people compared him to the handsome athlete Rick Fox.

Steve started off caring and didn't care for white or light women, as far as I could tell. Having sex with Steve gave me the feeling that I had been young and dumb because — I had no clue that the penetration part of sex was supposed to feel phenomenal as well. I was under the impression that only oral sex felt good, and it had started to get boring.

Steve was very tall and skinny, but his penis had a personality all of its own when I was on top of him during sex. I imagined that this must have been what it felt like to be on top of the Eiffel Tower. The first time Steve and I had sex, my legs shook uncontrollably for an hour. I wasn't sure what was happening, but after a couple of times, I was convinced great sex was the source. Steve and his family welcomed me and my two children with open arms and never made us feel anything less than family.

It wasn't long before I was married and pregnant with my third child. Only this time, I could be happy. Steve and I didn't have much, but he knew how to make me feel loved. Steve may not have liked white or light women, but he surely liked dark women, and I mean lots of them.

I had started to question Steve's loyalty a couple of months into my pregnancy. Of course, being back in Montgomery, Steve drove the popular Chevy Caprice much like the one that had once been driven by Lorenzo during our relationship. Once again, the popularity of this car would yet again prove to be problematic for me.

Steve started staying out later and not picking up his phone. It seemed he too, had a representative. He even became aggressive, which gave me enough red flags to do a little investigating of my own.

One night, Steve decided not to check in or answer his phone. I was very familiar with the parts of town he favored and decided to give them a look. Just as I was about to resign as an investigator, I spotted his Chevy Caprice on 24's parked right in front of room 4-B. Just like when I was pregnant and alone with Emerald, it would be happening yet again, feeling like deja vu.

Me and Steve would reconcile but the once Steamy Steve was now on ice. He was no longer affectionate but had become abusive. At this point I didn't know who Steve was anymore and despite our marriage no longer resembling longevity, I tried my hardest to keep our family together. Steve knew exactly how to pick a fight that would result in him storming out, which usually was a reason for him to be with other women.

After an invasive surgery, I didn't have the energy to fight with Steve. I could tell he had other plans. I really just wished he'd leave versus picking a fight. I attempted to do everything to avoid arguing with Steve that night because – the surgery to remove an abscess on my head had been stressful enough and was causing my head to ache.

I walked to a nearby neighbor's house, which only made matters worse. Steve only followed behind me in his rage. Steve no longer wanted to pick a fight; he wanted to fight, and he decided to take more action by pushing me to the ground.

Then, while I was on the ground, he grabbed me by my hair, dragging me, as the older gentleman next door yelled out for him to release me. I could barely get up off the ground as tears just rolled down my face. I wasn't only embarrassed, I was hurt physically and emotionally.

Steve did several more disturbing things. There was one other incident where he shot a gun at me. The bullet was lodged into the wall, which stopped inches away from my baby in the next room. I wanted so badly to make my marriage work but once he had become negligent enough to almost hurt my kid, that was where I drew the line, and much like a cake baked with missing ingredients, the damage was done.

What was once known as the Cooks was done as well. Lorenzo would eventually come back to recover what was left of his family, which I was all for, except for us being together. I was all over the place at this point. I just needed a break from men.

Lorenzo was more than willing to help me and the kids move back to Tennessee until he realized I was very serious about us not being together. This would be a choice that turned me into Super Mom, and that made me face the realization that – I was once again alone. My life was somewhat shaken up again, working at a burger joint and trying to raise three kids, all while back on public transportation.

Lorenzo and his parents didn't come

from North Tennessee to help me too often. Lorenzo always said he didn't have a ride, and his parents were too boogie to come to the 'hood' as they called, where me and the kids lived to help me out. I was able to repair my car and life was beginning to feel somewhat normal; even with me and Lorenzo not speaking due to one of our many fallouts.

Lorenzo and I had learned to be great co-parents and even friends. He even volunteered to keep Steve's son in exchange for the convenience of me bringing the kids on an hour-away drive to Clarksvillie due to him not having a car. The fallout between us would be much more extreme this time. Lorenzo and I had fallen out due to me stopping his visitations with the kids because of my knowledge of him selling drugs out of the same apartment where he kept the kids. After months of Lorenzo and I not speaking, I would receive a knock at the door.

The kids were always sure not to answer the door but instead tell me if someone was there. I had no clue of who would be knocking at my door. I remained quiet until the visitor walked off; once they walked away, I had no doubt of who the knocker was. "Lorenzo," I yell out!

Lorenzo's walk was one of a kind. It was quite unique and he could be spotted miles away because of it. Lorenzo turned around and pulled back the hood portion of his hoodie, and as he began to walk in my direction. I wondered if I should have been reluctant to open the door because this could very well be part two of our dispute.

Once Lorenzo was in front of me, he would hand me a large roll of money, and an apology would follow. He then stressed to me that he had changed and was indeed going to do better. Honestly, by looking at the BMW and the amount of cash that Lorenzo had on a Dollar Store salary, his life as a drug dealer was moving in the direction of a horrifying end.

Just in time for the Christmas holiday, I had no money. Lorenzo and Ebenezer Scrooge were now one and the same with their ability to save Christmas. Lorenzo suggested that we spend Christmas with his parents, which I agreed to.

I must admit, his parents could be cool at times as long as something was in it for them and it didn't involve them giving anything. His parents desperately were trying to appear as the Huxtables; now that — everyone was made aware of their leprosy. It was made public knowledge about the couple's now adult daughter, who had been given away at birth.

I admit Lorenzo's parents' home would be so pleasant and full of love and laughter around the holidays which made the kids happy. There was more than enough food and alcohol, and the look of the Christmas tree was phenomenal. Lorenzo's mom had this weird obsession with the game Charade and wouldn't let Christmas go by without dragging us all into the living room area to play our hearts out.

After a couple of alcoholic beverages, Lorenzo's mom didn't have to try too hard to get us to play at that point because – we were all tipsy, and to us all, it was going to be a good night. Things were starting to feel too right, but I didn't question God's plan. I would soon find out why a good feeling made me feel suspicious.

Lorenzo's sister would call me early one Sunday morning. All I could hear was their mom screaming in the background. The kids had spent the night with them, and all I could think was, please don't tell me something happened to my kids. She demanded that I come there, and I replied, "Only after you have told me why."

Lorenzo's sister would tell me that he was dead from a fatal gunshot to his heart during an attempted robbery. Although me and Lorenzo weren't in a sexual relationship anymore, we had learned how to love each other without the sex; and besides, we had two children together. That day, a part of me did die, and being left alone with kids was starting to feel all too familiar to me.

CHAPTER

Losing Lorenzo really hurt. Even though in my opinion our relationship was a typical R. Kelly and Aaliyah story, two children had come out of it, which made our story a bit more painful. I honestly didn't think I would ever get over the amount of hurt I was feeling after Lorenzo died. He was a big part of my past, and our two kids would make him a part of my future even if he wasn't physically there.

Lorenzo's parents became even more distant than they had been before. They always gave the same excuse, "Your mom doesn't answer her phone," or the classic one from his mom, "It hurts to see the kids. They look too much like Lorenzo." Lorenzo's parents didn't owe me anything, so I couldn't blame them for my situation. I just wished they'd be honest and not make the kids think it was me.

Lorenzo didn't have a living will. Legally, all his belongings should have been given to his children. But it wouldn't have been Lorenzo's mom if she had done the human thing.

She instead divided all his belongings amongst his brothers. Lorenzo didn't have anything I wanted, but the only working tv in our house would go out shortly after Lorenzo's death. You would think at least his kids would be entitled to his tv, but not if his mom had anything to do with it.

I quickly grew tired of Lorenzo's parents' lies, and I decided I would be just as distant as they were. And although they never called my phone, they were now officially on block. They would need to call Emerald's phone, which they should have initially done anyway.

At this point, my life was becoming darker by the day. I was still crying myself to sleep nightly. I was all alone in a big city with three kids. I continued putting as much as I could into life, although I felt empty most days.

I just wanted to finish the day so I could do it all again the next day. I knew if I wanted better for me and my kids something had to change, and it had to change fast. I would eventually pull myself together and obtain my General Education Diploma, which was something Lorenzo was helping me to achieve before he passed away.

Crying myself to sleep at night would continue until I met Jeremy. He seemed to be nice enough and interested in me for all the right reasons. When I met Jeremy, he had just as much as I did, if not more, and was as much as I believed I could ask from a man being that I had three children.

I quickly learned that my eggs turned down no sperm even though we used condoms. I still managed to get pregnant. After the baby, I didn't see Jeremy that often, which didn't bother me. It was normal for me at this point to not have a man around. I had become okay knowing I may never meet Mr. Right.

Jeremy didn't do a whole lot for our baby Gabriel, but I still allowed him to come over for an occasional hook-up, "Yeah, I know, stupid, right?" It would be during one of these hookups that I would solve the mystery of how I managed to get pregnant so fast. This bastard was poking holes in the condoms. I couldn't believe what I was seeing: a pinhole right through the wrapper. I wanted to kill him, but the damage had already been done.

I didn't want to be a victim. But it seemed no matter how hard I tried, life continued to throw me down. Of course, I could've done more to prevent getting pregnant, but never would I ever think someone would intentionally want a baby with me. Once I learned more about Jeremy's history, it all made sense.

He was a serial reproductive abuser, and unfortunately, I just so happened to have been in his path. However, Gabriel was a happy, healthy child, and she would grow right before my eyes. "Mama," she would always say due to the fact she never knew of any other authority figure in the home. When Gabriel was about three, my home girl, Keisha would convince me to join a dating app. She insisted it was what I needed.

She didn't put a gun to my head, and at any minute, I could have objected. But being that the last two years had been pure loneliness and two fingers, I chose to give it a try against my better judgment. "Left, Left," I swiped. Everyone was only interested in sex. I entertained a couple of guys for fun and even went out on a date or two with one guy; being long distance. It was cool, but nothing ever came of it.

Me and Marcus talked for about six months. Marcus was handsome and, I mean handsome, but he had a bit of a temper. It was never shown toward me, but his baby mama could get it at any moment, which meant if we continued to talk, it could eventually become me. I don't even remember how we ended, but we did.

And just like that, I was back at square one. I didn't give up on the app. I decided to keep swiping until one day, I stopped, and there he was.

Fabulous was light-skinned and he wore a hat. That's it, that's all, and he wasn't from Nasvillie,TN, which was all I really needed to know or cared about. Fabulous and I would talk many nights, and he appeared to be a nice and charming guy who cracked jokes to make me laugh.

We would meet for the first time at Keisha's house. Knock, knock, "Who is it?" He replied, "Fabulous," in those short seconds, my mind told me millions of times not to answer. I opened the door, and there he was. Only this time, there was no hat, just light skin and big lips.

Once inside, he would go on and on about his baby mamas and children, which would be a total turn-off right along with his farther back than usual hairline. Even though I didn't like his appearance, his ambition did mean something. He had the drive to become an HVAC Technician by any means necessary.

Much like Ciara felt about Russell Wilson, Fabulous wasn't what I was used to, but he was what I had assumed I needed. Although, our story was missing celebrity status and money. His charm would grow on me and eventually win me over. I allowed him inside of my hurting, broken body.

Physically, my body didn't hurt, but due to the many unworthy spirits that I allowed to have possession over my body and call it theirs, it was indeed hurt, broken, and crying out for help. Fabulous would move to Tennessee with a dream but he was not quite sure of how he would execute it. Fabulous spent most nights at my house, and even though I had been intimate with him, I was still not ready to introduce him to my kids.

Chapter 12

I was always sure to have Fabulous out by 6:00am to beat the kids waking up. Fabulous and I seemed to be moving pretty fast. Before I knew it, he was no longer beating the kids out the door in the mornings.

Fabulous delivered cleaning supplies until he was accepted into the HVAC program. But still, he was always sure to keep me in mind, making sure to bring me something or take me out in his spare time. It wasn't long before this fairy tale started turning into a nightmare, although I was wide awake.

Fabulous would eventually become very needy. He needed a place to stay, a car, and even though we had only been in a relationship for three months, I wanted to make it work. I decided to help Fabulous and thought he would do the right thing.

As far as I knew, he never gave me credit for basically allowing a stranger to borrow my car and giving him a roof over his head. No way was I going to let Fabulous' ungrateful ass break my spirit. I was in the process of building a stable life for myself and my kids.

The first of the year was always full of cheer at my house. One reason was because most of the household was Aquarius. I also got the good news that I had been approved to close on my first home. It had appeared that I had been too prepared for bad weather lately. My gut was telling me I would soon be caught in a storm without my umbrella.

Less than a week after being approved to close on my home, I would receive a disturbing call that would turn my smile upside down. Fabulous would call to say his brother had shot himself in the chest. My boss and I were at odds. So, unfortunately, if I wanted to secure a future for us, I would need to stay those thirty more minutes and act as if everything was okay. I soon arrived at the hospital to witness a waiting room full of people talking and laughing, trying not to think of the young man who was fighting for his life ten doors down.

I was not able to stay very long because – I had to work the next morning. So, after about two hours, I said my goodbyes and headed toward the parking deck. On day four, I would return to the hospital to support Fabulous, only to find out there had not been any changes in his brother's condition.

I had never had a chance to officially meet Scott, Fabulous' brother. This would be the first time I would meet him; although he wouldn't remember it. It was one meet and greet that I would never forget.

It was time for Fabulous to say his good-byes and I took the walk hand-in-hand with him. As we passed the ninth door, I took a deep breath to prepare myself because I had no clue of what I was going to see. This could very well be the one time in Fabulous's life when he showed an ounce of emotion and broke down.

Once we entered the room, I saw a man that had given up. Even though so many wanted him to stay, he had other plans. His body lay there covered in tattoos, but Scott was no longer there. He was in transition wherever that may have been, so I guess I can say I really never met him.

Scott would die the next morning due to the removal of his life support and no change in his condition. I didn't know much about Fabulous' brother except what I had heard and on the outside, looking in. He managed to keep his family together and was the whole reason for Fabulous' interest in being an HVAC Technician. Going off what little information I had, I would call him a good man.

It was more than I could say for Fabulous. If he had to explain, he'd say his brother only got as far as he did off his family's money, which wasn't Fabulous family due to them having different moms. With three kids, he paid child support for two and only saw them once every three to five years.

I would call him out on that often and demand that he do better. The demands on top of the lack of support he stressed I showed when his brother died; we were just spread too thin. Before the summer could come in he would be out and back to freely being himself.

I would love to say I was relieved when we finally broke up, but I did miss him. And not because he was just all that but because – I had grown to love him. Life slowly moved on, and I learned to become busy. I was making more money without him than I made with him.

The kids and I took two vacations, but I honestly cannot say I was satisfied. I would reach out to Fabulous, and he seemed happy to hear from me. I never told him I missed him. I just made up some story about him having clothes left at the house, and we should meet up so he could retrieve them.

We would meet and not say more than two words to each other and that is where I should have left it. Knowing that I loved him but didn't want him confused me. I knew my heartbeat didn't match his at this point. I was beginning to think I may not be a match for anyone.

The thought of me being back here again made me feel defeated, which wasn't new for me. "Why didn't I just stay single?" I had been through so much, and it seemed that any setback, no matter how small, had begun to make me question God and foresee death as an easier option.

Lately, I had been in the presence of a different me. When I looked into the mirror, the reflection of me now revealed a broken soul on the verge of a break. I had cried out too long; the results were the same. I was feeling insane. My soul was seeping from my body faster than air from a tire needing repair.

CHAPTER 13

I fought daily with colorism at work, in relationships, and even with family. But no matter how hard I tried to escape, it always found me and took me a few steps back. My life wasn't the best, but I was beginning to think I could possibly beat this thing. I was no longer going to be a victim. At this point, I had at least taken care of one of the problems that was causing me to struggle in life: money.

I had done my due diligence, and money was less of a problem. I did need a budget being that I had just purchased my first home. Dentistry was my new profession after enduring the pain of losing my first patient. I knew nursing wasn't for me, especially because – that was a common thing in nursing. I couldn't face the fact that it could potentially happen again. I must admit working around only women all day was putting me right back in that dark space, which I was determined to stay away from.

As a dark-skinned woman, I never felt good enough in this profession due to the women always being in competition. With me usually being the darkest in the building, no matter what I did, I was considered dead last. Having a big butt these days made–you the shit and could maybe gain a darker woman a point or two.

If there was a light female with this feature, however, that dark one could just forget about it. In my case, I was dark, and my hair and makeup weren't within the budget, so I wasn't even noticed in anyone's peripheral view. I did have one thing that made me a little tolerable, which was my jokes.

I could make people laugh which was the only reason my attendance was wanted. No one ever took my jokes personally. I assumed it was due to the aggression and combativeness that were said to be a characteristic of the dark-skinned woman.

The doctors, on the other hand, only cared for my sense of humor half of the time, and even then, they only smiled. Not sure if humorlessness was taught in medical school; they never really laughed a lot no matter how much of a comedian I was. They still looked at me as a brown brown girl, who didn't mean shit in this world. So, for them, it was best I left the jokes to Kevin Hart.

My color wasn't marketable in any field. The only continent was maybe Africa, but even they looked for the accent for authenticity. Over the years, I had experienced my darker skin being frowned upon by blacks, only to have them pretend there was a rational explanation; when this has clearly been around since slavery. I would have been a field nigger based on my darker skin.

I had been fired on account of my skin, although those were never the words used. I had once been told I was aggressive, so my services would only be needed for two more weeks. "Two more weeks?" I vowed to never give another company that much power over me and I wouldn't allow myself to be made a mockery.

By the time I had reached my last dentist office, I was only interested in working part-time while me and Fabulous were broken up. I took that time to work on myself and started a business, which gave me another source of income. I no longer had to be the life of the party to fit in. The doctors still didn't treat me nearly as good as the lighter and white girls, and if it ever came down to my word against theirs, my alibi would need to be solid.

Three days a week, I dealt with women who looked at me as though I had failed in life because — I didn't look like them, and I had four kids. So, of course, I never answered the phone or came in on my off days to help. But this just left space open for Fabulous to try and find his way back in.

Honestly, I hated Fabulous and never should have entertained him. I had become a desperate woman, the woman that I had told my daughters not to be. Don't be a woman who settled for a piece of a man rather than wait for God to send a whole one.

Fabulous sent flowers to my job in a small red vase wrapped with a red and white ribbon, holding six red roses and a card that read, "To my Bama Mamma from Sugar Bear." This got the women talking, causing a frenzy. You can bet within the next two weeks, everyone was sending flowers to themselves and claiming it was from their boo. Sugar Bear was a name we had kind of come up with due to him being so hairy. He was covered with so much hair it could literally be braided to the back.

I allowed Fabulous to come over to the house. The kids were happy to see him, and I guess the flowers had turned my hateful heart back golden because I smiled a little when his car pulled up, too. My son remembered a rematch on Madden and demanded that Fabulous give it to him. Fabulous threw his phone on my bed. " Let's go," he said as he went back across the hall.

While Fabulous was busy taking a beat down from my son, his phone would not stop ringing. "Fab," "Yes Buttercup," he would sing as he walked into the room. "Your phone has been ringing since you've been here." Fabulous wasted no time confessing that he was in a relationship with multiple girls, and the one who was calling was a sixty-year-old woman who had no teeth. She really felt like she had hit the jackpot when she was able to pull him.

He explained that he had cut most of them off. But this one, Ms. Toothless just wouldn't give up. He revealed that she took care of him and even gave him a daily allowance. After she realized that he was really done, he had to return the bags of clothes and shoes which she had bought for him.

I was beginning to learn more and more about Fabulous. Although he claimed chocolate was his preference, he obviously had no type. He regularly quoted that big women paid like they weighed and, from looking at his phone, he would sleep with anyone.

I must admit, I wasn't too thrilled to hear about his activities, even though we weren't to-gether. I knew that he was a cheater. Looking at myself in the mirror made me take a step back. I would request that he leave due to his honesty. He would give the same look puppies give as you pass them in the pet shop.

I wasn't ready to buy and closed the door behind him as he gave me one last pitiful look. Once he was gone, I felt like I wanted him. I wanted to call him back cause I was sure he was going straight to one of the chicks who he hadn't quite scratched off the list, but I couldn't make myself do it.

As tears filled my eyes, I wondered to myself how did I get here with him. My cock-iness was brief, and I dropped onto the bed as my heart began to feel so weak. "Why couldn't God have made me just two shades lighter?" I was sure that the cruel treatment from family, men, and co-workers would've been different if only I were brighter. As I contemplated over my glum life, the pain became overwhelming, and my eyes shut.

CHAPTER 14

Fabulous would reenter my life faster than water gushing from a broken fire hydrant in Brooklyn. This time, he had come with energy resembling a vendetta. I had tried to convince myself that Fabulous had changed and he had cut all those women off for me.

The one who was giving him a daily allowance could even remove her teeth for better access to his dick. The second girl was weeks away from a cruise with him, all expenses paid. Funny, she would be the one he would reconnect with after leaving me that night. Manda was a girl that just wanted to fuck. She had even made plans for them to join a polyamory party, but he would miss this event all to return to plain old me.

Over time, Fabulous's intentions became clear, and I knew my suspicions were valid. He had resented me for giving up all the women. He still argued that I could have been there more for him when his brother died, which only pulled us farther apart. Fabulous didn't spend the night as much this time around.

But one night, he must have been feeling vulnerable. He decided to confide in me, which he had never done prior to this night. Fabulous would reveal to me that he had killed his father. He explained that his father was in so much pain that he insisted Fabulous turn up his meds to overdose and take him out of his misery.

This would be one conversation that would leave me speechless, all I wanted to do was play sleep. As I lay there, I ignored Fabulous' attempts to wake me so that my cover wasn't blown. I thought to myself, could I kill one of my parents? I concluded I couldn't do it even if they asked. I wouldn't be able to live with myself.

I tried to imagine how Fabulous must have felt being asked to do such a horrific task. Then I thought to myself, what if his dad had doubts as the meds were slowly moving through his veins and body, and he no longer could
114

signal for a change of heart due to his life slowly leaving his body? What if Fabulous acted as a villain and killed his dad due to his exhaustion from being his caregiver?

I had no clue of the circumstances. All I knew was that – Fabulous had just confessed to overdosing his dad. He somehow felt justified because – his dad was already suffering from cancer, heart disease, and a few other illnesses.

After that night, it became even harder to look at Fabulous, not that we didn't already have enough chaos in the relationship despite all that being revealed. If I continued to be with the killer, maybe I had my own demons, which I was dealing with, which allowed me to overlook his. Fabulous, and I fussed often, I admit. It was hard for me to get over the many women that he had slept with; it only led me to question other situations that may have seemed suspicious.

During an argument, I stormed out, and I gave Fabulous the impression that I had met up with another guy. When I returned, Fabulous was gone. He had tried to contact me that night, but I wanted to seem as though I was up to no good and make him feel as I had so many times before. Once I did connect with Fabulous, I would learn my plan had backfired because –

Fabulous had indeed been intimate with some-one that night. He wasn't remorseful, which confirmed my suspicion that – he had never left the dating website and was just waiting on an opportunity to swipe.

This should have been the moment when I was done. But I had already by this time given Fabulous four years off and on. I wasn't as young anymore, and due to the way society was still degrading women of my shade, I decided to move forward and hope for the best.

The next month our world would face one of the biggest pandemics that had been seen. Many states had been shut down and even some countries. Fabulous, the kids and I were shut in for months. It brought us a little closer, and any opportunities to sneak off we did.

Fabulous' cousin had come into town, and he had made plans to meet up with him due to the overdue time from quarantining in the house. I was up for the outing as well. Fabulous' cousin would send his location, and we would arrive within an hour with smiles for a chance to unwind.

We would be greeted back with smiles as we approached the door. Fabulous' cousin was staying with a friend of his wife and she seemed pretty nice. Laughter would fill the room as we began to consume alcoholic beverages and make small talk. The conversation would take a detour as I began to talk about being a brown brown girl born in the South and the experiences I had genuinely that resulted from it.

Everyone in the room disagreed with my comments on colorism, and they would argue that all blacks were treated unjustly, which in return made me feel as though they were saying white lives matter. Of course, we know all lives matter. We also know that blacks are being killed just for the color of their skin alone, but that doesn't remove the fact that colorism exists amongst blacks.

I couldn't believe it. I was bullied and belittled, and Fabulous was the ringleader. He insisted on arguing that all brown people's experiences were pretty much the same, but what would he know with his light skin ass.

I couldn't say I was surprised. His cousin would try to help me by explaining his experience, and although he was of a lighter complexion, he was still the darkest member of his family. He had experienced the kind of hate that blacks inflicted on each other.

Fabulous wasn't convinced but high-fived the group as they continued to make me look stupid without caring for my feelings. I wasn't sharing theory; this was a first-hand experience for me. I grew exceedingly quiet. I usually wasn't at a loss for words, but at that moment, I knew I had been defeated.

This wasn't the first time Fabulous had allowed me to be disrespected. At times, it seemed to be his goal. I was aware that we were with his family, but at any time, he could've thrown in the ring buoy, but instead, he benefited from watching me drown.

On the way out, Fabulous hugged all the members of his clan, reassuring them that I was insane and that they were justified in breaking me down. The ride home was quiet. I had been humiliated not just by strangers but by a man who called himself my lover, my friend, my confidant, and my man.

My heart was so heavy, and I couldn't stop thinking about how he should have defended me. I shared my life experiences and my truth with this group, all to be ridiculed, and a contributor to the maltreatment was my man. He once said he loved me, and now here he was crushing my spirits.

Once we were in the driveway, I dismissed myself from the car and went straight for medicines containing diphenhydramine. Not sure if killing myself was the motive, but I was sure I didn't want to see Fabulous's face whether I lived or died. He was no longer someone I had a passion for.

CHAPTER

My mom and I hadn't spoken in a couple of months, which wasn't out of the norm for us. I figured what the heck, I had time on my hands, which I knew we'd need due to the lengthy conversation we'd have after this amount of time apart. "Hey mom," she replied, "Hey Nyla," she immediately began to cry.

"Oh Lord, Mom, don't start that," she began, trying to calm herself to keep me on the line. This was where my mom was supposed to tell me, "I'm still your mama and then ask how are the kids doing?" But she instead replied with, "I have to tell you something."

I could tell by the tone of her voice that whatever it was, it wasn't good but serious, if I may add. Her voice was cracking from trying to hold back tears; it was also consumed with sadness. I had never heard that coming from my mom.

"Nyla, I have breast cancer." I didn't cry. I knew my mom was a fighter. She had been there for my aunts through their sicknesses; surely, God was going to spare my mom's life. I didn't allow my mom to elaborate. I told her I would give her a callback and informed my family that – we would be taking a trip to Montgomery the next morning, so they needed to be ready.

We all loaded up into Fabulous' car because his car was bigger than mine. It was spacious enough to carry the six of us, and we began the four-hour drive. We stopped for gas and breakfast with hopes of this stop being the only one until we had reached our destination.

We made small talk along the way, but about an hour into it, everyone was asleep except me and Fabulous, which gave me great satisfaction. I really didn't have a desire to talk. I could only think about my mom.

My mom was surprised to see us once we arrived. I hadn't told her I was coming, only that – I would give her a callback. Everyone gave her a hug and kiss on the cheek.

We talked for a bit; then, my mom asked me to come into the living room area away from the others. She showed me her doctor's schedule, and then the big reveal was of her distorted left breast. She began to cry, but I assured her everything would be fine.

God knows I didn't want to lose my mom. I had already lost my dad years back while me and my dad weren't on speaking terms. Losing him was hard enough, but moms were different, indeed totally different.

She didn't care that my skin was dark. She had no agenda for loving me. She loved me for my existence and that alone. Despite my sister's determination to disperse rumors about her and my now-dead baby's father being together, we had remained close and always said if our mom ever got sick, we'd drop everything to move back home and care for her.

Having a family of my own, I knew that was no longer an option, but I wasn't going to leave my mom out to dry. I had to figure something out and the best thing I could think of was bringing my mom to live with me. Fabulous was all about healthy living. He had researched Dr. Sebi and learned to eat healthy, but he also learned to be a womanizer, with Dr. Sebi's promotion for having many women. I needed to run the idea across to my mom first – even though I felt she would object to staying with me and my rambunctious crew. I needed to do my due diligence before I could come to that conclusion.

The conversation between my mom and I would be short. She expressed the need to inform her husband, and I agreed that was the right thing to do. Upon calling me back, my mom would deliver the news that she would be staying in her own home, and her husband had assured her that he would care for her. Who was I to argue with their decision? It wasn't long after that that my mom would have her first chemo treatment and me and my two sisters, along with my Aunt April, accompanied her.

Due to Covid, my mom would have to take the fiercest and scariest walk of her life all alone. As my mom entered the building with her head hung low, I remembered thinking that God knew all. While I was battling with my pigmented appearance and whether I wanted to live, my mom was actually fighting for her life as she so desperately wanted more of it.

Chapter 15

My oldest sister Kizzy had stepped up higher than I had ever expected her to. She would call to fuss at me. I never took it to heart because I knew she must have been over-whelmed being the only daughter my mom had residing in the same state as her.

Kizzy and I noticed the need for more help for our mom, so we quickly organized a conference call with our Aunt April in hopes that she would be on board to help us out. Aunt April was more than willing to help, as she had cared for so many others in their times of need and had already been a huge part of my mom's health decision-making process. It only made sense that we confided in her.

I promised my mom that I would come down as much as possible, with Fridays being the priority day. Fridays were her Chemo days and it was important to me that she saw at least one of her kids in her corner, even if we couldn't enter the facility with her. When it came time to discuss Fridays off with the dentist I worked for, she wouldn't be pleased. Being that we had ini-tially agreed on me working this day, she politely declined my request and terminated me.

I was thankful for the previous vow I had made to myself of never allowing any company to have control over me. So when the doctor dismissed me, I graciously walked away with my head held high. I knew I would be able to spend what could potentially be my mom's last days with her.

Even though I was prepared for the dismissal, I can't say that I didn't think about the way this job and others had unapologetically treated me just because they could. The departure incident only made me think back to the day Fabulous allowed me to be drastically disrespected. You see – part of their argument was that blacks needed to hire their own, but where did that leave me?

I thought. I was not amongst the marketable shade. So when Fabulous protested that we hire our own, I still didn't meet the criteria. When I did, I still wasn't equal to everyone else. Fabulous' method might have been logical for him being a lighter complexion individual, but for a brown brown individual like me, it meant nothing.

I understood that there was nothing I could do about employers, or anyone for that matter, not being fond of darker-skinned individuals. I must say it frustrated me, and I felt like a knife was being pushed deeper and deeper into me each time. I was faced with the hate from my own people. I was tired of hearing employers say it's just business because — in my book, that statement didn't make them exempt from being human; and as adults, they knew right from wrong.

My travel to Montgomery would soon be upped to two days a week quickly. Kizzy had used up her vacation days at the beginning of my mom's discovery of her illness, and she requested I be accessible to assist with our mom's care when my brother couldn't or my cousin had to work. It wouldn't be long before Quay and her two daughters moved in and helped with the care of our mom which cut down on Kizzy's missed time from work as well as my travel.

Still, I wanted to do as much as I could to make my mom as comfortable as possible. Fabulous and I visited the health food store and picked up my mom a couple of items to help with her aches and pains. We had to make a late-night trip to deliver them since I had signed up for a driving class that was due to start the following Monday.

This trip would reveal that my mom's condition was taking a turn for the worse. My mom would make statements that night that gave the impression she was having memory loss, but I just took note of it. Maybe it was nothing, although it would be material that she should have had knowledge of.

On the drive home, my mom's memory loss was all I could think about. Fabulous could care less. He was probably just hoping I was gracious enough to treat him for his beyond-kind gesture of bringing me to see my sick mother.

Fabulous, and I still wasn't seeing eye to eye at this time. I thought he would have a little mercy on me, being that my mom wasn't in the best shape. But judging by the way he treated me when I was going through something, he probably thought I deserved it.

My mom had decorated for years parties, weddings, and birthdays; from making bows and wreaths to hats, she did it. Hell, our house won best Christmas decoration for six years in a row. So I knew she'd want to be a part of her own funeral arrangements if it came down to that. I knew I needed to have that conversation with my mom while she was still able to speak for herself.

I knew the conversation would be hard, but as my mom truly loved to make each event special, I was sure she would want nothing less. She would want to select the colors, the flowers, her clothes, and casket for her last event. The next morning, I made the call to my mom, "Hey, Mom."

"Hey, Nyla," I just came right out with it. She was appreciative and strong. She didn't cry, although I knew she was scared shitless. I knew lilies were my mom's favorite flower, and beige was her favorite color.

And just as I had thought, those were the exact colors she pointed out for the casket and flowers, along with the clothes she wanted to wear. My mom met with an insurance adjuster later that week, accompanied by my Aunt April. We had been on a three-way phone call for all other arrangements. Why not this one, I thought?

Me and my mom were mad often, but when we were speaking, we talked about everything. Even what was to take place at this meeting, so I didn't even bother putting up a fight. After the meeting was over it appeared my mom did not have as much money as she thought she had.

Apparently, my mom only had enough money to cover her funeral expenses and leave her grandchildren with a couple hundred dollars. At least, that was the information given to my sister Kizzy. By the end of the week, my mom was back at the hospital, only this time she was admitted.

My mom and I spoke on the phone, and she confirmed due to COVID she was very much alone with no one to talk to or interact with, which was not helping her condition. "Mom, you are not alone," I tried to reassure her. My mom knew the Lord and she knew exactly what I meant. "You are free of distractions; it's just you and God." At that moment, she seemed to have received a bit of peace.

Back in Tennessee, I felt helpless because I wished there was more that I could have done to help my mom. It was bad enough that the "Bitch Cancer" was messing with my mom, but a new Bitch had come to help COVID–and neither of them were letting up. My cousin was scheduled to drop my mom's phone off, so I encouraged him to download as many games as possible on her phone to keep her occupied. I couldn't help but think there was something my Aunt April wasn't telling me, and I needed to know what it was. I needed to have a conversation with her, so I called her.

"Hey, April," I said when April picked up the phone. "Is my mom going to die?" I had never heard my Aunt April cry, not even at a funeral. She was always the strongest.

As soon as the words left my mouth, she began to cry uncontrollably. I could tell by April's reaction that she either knew the answer to the question I had just asked her or she believed it. Either way, it was bad, and at that moment, my soul checked out of my body, leaving a mess behind.

CHAPTER

I could only pray that my mom was receiving the best care without being able to see her for myself. Due to COVID, no one was allowed into the hospital. I hadn't seen much of my mom, and it had been about two days since I last spoke to her.

My dad's sister worked at the hospital and was able to give me an update on my mom's condition; she was even able to obtain a number that I used to Facetime my mom. Immediately, I called to speak to her, and although it seemed like hell on the outside, but on the inside, my mom appeared to be in good spirits. "Hey, Mom," she replied back, "Hey, stranger," as she smiled.

I could tell she was happy to see a familiar face. Nurses were right in the middle of taking my mom to have some test run, so we wrapped up with I love you. I assured her that I'd be speaking to her the next day. I was so thrilled that I could now see my mom and not have to assume how she was being treated.

I didn't want to overwhelm the nurses but I did want to talk to my mom more. The next morning, I called, and the nurse said that my mom wasn't doing too well; she couldn't talk and was only moaning. "Are you sure we're referring to the same patient?" I asked.

"Yes," she replied to my question. At this time, the nurse wasn't sure if I still wanted to see her being in the state that my mom was in. I had just talked to my mom the day before, and she was happy, so she could definitely talk. I needed to see her. I was in disbelief and insisted that the nurse still let me see my mother.

The nurse called out to my mom, "Mrs. Patterson." I could only hear her moaning. I demanded that she get closer; indeed, it was my mother. What could have happened within that short amount of time? After that day my mom had stopped talking and was not opening her eyes. She managed to force out a word here and there, but overall, she was mute.

Due to the nature of my mom's condition, doctors were allowing my mom to have two visitors at a time from close family. My baby brother PJ and his wife had just come in off the road, so they took the first visit. Kizzy called me to be present for the doctor's exam the next day with Quay and our Aunt, April.

The doctors thought that radiation treatment would be beneficial for my mom and encouraged us to make a decision. However, this was pretty much all they could do for her now. The doctors would be rolling my mom's bed into the treatment area due to her inability to walk anymore.

Kizzy asked my feelings on the treatment, and I felt strongly that my mom needed to come home to be with her family and let God take the wheel. After we all had a chance to talk amongst ourselves, we unanimously decided that my mom would be coming home with hospice. Fabulous and I traveled to Montgomery to visit my mom even though she wasn't due to be released until the following day.

I knew I didn't want to miss an opportunity. The hospital still needed to arrange for a bed to be delivered to her home. Kizzy and I had been communicating during my travels. She would be the second person present in the room while I was visiting my mom.

As soon as I pulled into the parking lot of the hospital, my heartbeat speeded up. The thought that I could possibly be losing my mom became all too real. On the way up to my mom's room, I convinced myself to calm down. Due to all my face gear, shades, and the new one, face-mask thanks to COVID, I was able to hide my fear behind them.

My sister had no idea I had been balling my eyes out when I entered the room. "Hey, mom," the usual "Hey, Nyla" from my mom fol-lowing my greeting was no more. As I got closer to my mom, I grabbed her hand. I could sense she knew I was there.

As she mostly moaned, I felt the need to comfort her, and I asked my mom, who had the last say? With all her energy, she replied, "God." I must admit I was, in return, comforted by the reply my mom made. I said, "I love you," and exited the room. I stopped by my mom's house before I headed back to Tennessee to confirm that her bed had been delivered. My brother Pj and his wife were present at the entrance of my mom's home when my stepdad Wiley walked up from the back and greeted me with a dry "hello."

My sister Quay was making the bed that had just been delivered by the hospital. The tension in the house was thicker than the fog traveling across San Francisco's Golden Gate Bridge on a morning in July due to the different alliances formed among the family. It was indeed evident that I had just stepped into uncharted territories.

Fabulous was planning to drive to Ohio at the end of the week to attend his youngest daughter Tyler's birthday party, who he hadn't seen in almost three years. The visit was beyond overdue. I had just completed my driving class, and the test to obtain my license was kicking my butt on top of school and the stress of my mom's life slipping away. I needed a getaway, even if it was with Fabulous.

On the drive to Ohio, I couldn't stop thinking about my mom. And although there was still some tension, me and Quay had put our differences aside for the moment to communicate again for the sake of our mom. Fabulous was going on and on about his old stomping grounds the entire ride. He needed to kill a little time, being that he couldn't get in touch with his daughter.

He drove the whole city, pointing out his old residents, schools, and former job sites. Fabulous was just getting back in the car after purchasing a pizza he had sworn by when his phone rang, "Thank God." Not sure if it was the stress, but I was sick of driving around hearing about his past life and was happy as hell his daughter had finally called with the location.

After Fabulous got the call from Tyler, he began driving to her party, which I admit seeing him excited made me smile. I often argued with Fabulous about the poor job he was doing with his children with the hope it would make him do better. Years would go by without him seeing his daughters.

Fabulous always found the nerve to complain about the horrible job his youngest child, Tyler's mother, was doing raising her. In my book, this was just downright disrespectful. Fabulous' daughter had once been taken by the state, and he felt the need to express how much it was her mother's fault.

Sure, a woman should have her man's back, but I felt it would have been a disservice to agree with Fabulous. For the simple fact that even if you factored in the maybe $300 dollars a year he pays, she was technically taking care of their child alone. So, with that being the case, I had to disagree with him. The night Fabulous' daughter was taken by the State, I was prepared to hold him as he cried himself to sleep but this was not the case. Fabulous slept like a baby that night and never lost a wink of sleep the entire time his daughter was in State custody.

Once we arrived at Tyler's grandmother's house where Tyler now stayed due to the State's refusal to give the child back to the mother. Fabulous had no idea of which of the apartment doors to knock on. After he had knocked on the first door, the tenant was able to direct Fabulous in the right direction.

Fabulous knocked, and the grandmother yelled, "It's your dad." His daughter would warm up to him about an hour after all her cousins and uncles showed up. One of Tyler's uncles had a white girlfriend, and it was very annoying that nigger was her choice of word whenever she needed to address her own son.

It was mind-boggling how Fabulous had been so vocal about racism, yet this white woman kept repeating nigger over and over, and that didn't bother him the least bit. It was about the third-nigger-in where I felt the need to dismiss myself and headed to the car. I needed to check on my mom anyway.

I had been very present with my mom's overall care.Being that me and Quay were now texting, she also informed me of all visitors coming if they didn't do so themselves. Quay had just texted me, letting me know how she was losing her patience with our brother Cory.

Cory was the brother that didn't give a fuck. He did and said what he wanted and was usually at odds with us all. He had a one-man alliance and wished a nigga would. My cousin Tiara had just given me a call to update me of her estimated arrival time, so I put her on duty to watch Cory.

My Aunt April usually came around this time and should have been arriving shortly. Between the two of them, peace would have been maintained to give Quay a break. Cory had left by the time Tiara had arrived, and April was still en route, but she was accompanied by one of my mom's girlfriends for her visit.

When Tiara entered the living room (that had now been made my mom's new living space), Kay, my mom's girlfriend was kneeling and holding her hand. Tiara took a seat and remained quiet, giving Kay time to finish her prayer. April had arrived and headed to my mother's side.

Once she was in the room, she immediately noted something was wrong. April pushed past Kay as she noticed the color of my mom's skin was now resembling that of a brown, brown girl rather than the beautiful light skin that she had once possessed. Quay had sent me a text that read Mom was no longer here.

Without hesitation, I called Quay as my Aunt April was still attempting to provide life-saving procedures, but there was nothing she could do. "Nyla, she is gone." Moms weren't supposed to die; I mean, moms were like super-heroes. How could this be happening? At that moment, I realized that both the people responsible for my existence were now deceased. From the speeding of my pulse, I could soon be gone, too.

CHAPTER

Fabulous showed no emotion when I informed him that my mother had passed away; however, he did make it a point to tell me I shouldn't have come anyway. I wanted to go be with my family, but we were in Fabulous' car. He wasn't ready to leave, and looked me in my face and said, "What's leaving going to do? You can't bring her back."

After about a two-hour wait, Fabulous finally gave in to my request, and we then embarked on a journey closer toward my worst nightmare. Fabulous, basically argued that the only reason for my interest in making this trip was to make sure he didn't relapse with some of his old female friends. At that moment, that pizza that Fabulous had sworn by was finally made good when I made a courtesy delivery of it to his face.

We argued the first three hours of the drive back home before reality kicked in; she was gone. The lady who had given me life was now lifeless. The words Fabulous had spoken, "You can't bring her back," had just hit me harder than Muhammad Ali's fist after he had strategically allowed his opponent to hit him over and over to tire them out, and he came back for the win.

Although I hated to admit that what Fabulous had said was right, I couldn't bring her back. Once we made it to Tennessee, I had already informed Fabulous that he needed to go. He grabbed some items from the house and left promptly after our arrival. I was exhausted from all the arguing, sleepless nights, and ride home; I laid down to nap, but my mind was telling a different story.

As I lay there, I could only replay memories of my mom. The only sense I could make of my mom's early departure was that God needed her more, which at the time was not satisfying. "Fuck it, let's go," me and the kids gathered in the car and headed toward Montgomery to make my mom's funeral arrangements.

Chapter 17

Once I entered the city of Montgomery, I stopped and got food for the family and headed to the house my mom had lived in for so many years and died. When I turned down my mom's street, cars seemed to stretch from my mom's house to the front of the neighborhood due to people wanting to pay their respects. "This is really happening," I cried the whole way down, so the kids didn't even bother asking if I was okay at this point.

The yard was filled with family and friends, and although the scenery was active, I had to get to the living room to see it for myself. There was plenty of small talk being made when I entered the house as I continued straight through the den and into the living room, which was dark and quiet. My mom's bed had been removed, and there was open space, but it was real. "She was really gone." I took a seat on the floor, looked up, and asked the question, "Why my mama?"

Emerald and I had started working on my mom's obituary as we waited for my Aunt April to show up to discuss a meeting at the funeral home; she was the beneficiary of the life insurance policy. We all agreed that noon would be an appropriate time to meet the following day to make the arrangements. I spent the night at

Kizzy's house to avoid the crowd at my mom's. Everyone was on time for once except Kizzy, of course. I loved my sister, but if she was on time, it would have been weird.

Aunt April led the way because – she was very familiar with funeral arrangements. So much so, that we just followed her lead because she in fact had all my mom's insurance money. "Well, hello April," she was greeted with a warm welcome; it gave a real Dave Ruffin and what's their name type of feel. We all were led by the secretary into a conference room to wait for the director to show us around and make our selections for my mom. We chose a casket rather fast because my mom had left detailed instructions behind on how her service should look.

When all selections had been made, the director escorted us back into the conference room to discuss money, where my oldest brother had joined in on the discussion. I wasn't sure what had changed, but the energy was different when we reentered the conference room. My mom and I had had the conversation years back about what–should happen with her insurance money if something were ever to happen to her, but I gave April the benefit of the doubt because – I knew she loved my mom.

146

I believed she would never do anything to hurt my mom or us. My mom was certain all those years ago that she wanted Kizzy to make her funeral arrangements and split the remainder of the funds amongst her children. I was left to assume that the energy shift was due to my mom's husband, eldest child, and even my oldest brother, who were all alive and well, yet April had still been left in charge. We watched as my Aunt April made the final decisions on what was and not to be purchased with my mom's insurance money.

It was strange that the day after my mom had met with the insurance adjuster. We were informed that the cancer had spread to her brain. Raising the question if my mom was even of sound mind? And if not, how would my aunt have known what my mom wishes really were?

Quay and Joseph, my cousin who my mom took in after his mother passed, both stayed in the car while we visited the funeral home. PJ and Cory didn't attend, so my step-dad, Kizzy, Tay, and myself were the only family members present to assist April in the decision-making process. COVID wasn't letting up and was continuing to make our life hell every step of the way.

The funeral director was willing to assign us family cars, but only four people could sit in a car. That was a problem because my mom had a husband with six kids and a bonus child. She also had eighteen grandchildren, so the number of cars April was willing to pay for just wouldn't have accommodated us all.

We had no idea how much the insurance check was for, so we didn't know what my mom could afford. Later that day, Kizzy contacted her and my mom's pastor. We were sure my mom would have wanted all her family together in one building and not the service everyone else was providing their loved ones due to the COVID-19 virus. We knew we had to at least make the call to her pastor.

My mom was a loyal member of her church, so Kizzy asked if we could host my mom's service there. Her pastor replied, "yes' ' without hesitation. As a member, it was free of charge, and although many other families were strongly practicing burial-side services to allow social distancing, with the help of my mom's church, we were still able to maintain that same distance, all while fulfilling my mom's wishes.

The next day, Kizzy, Quay, and I needed to order the lilies to cover the casket my mom was quite specific about. The cream colored lilies ended up being white, we were determined to come as close as possible. The florist did inform us that she could provide lilies, although several of them would not have bloomed, and it would be wise if we selected a flower to fill the open spaces.

Kizzy was thinking of what flower would work, being that – my mom had only spoken of lilies. While Quay had remained quiet, at that moment, it came to me. I remembered that PJ's father always bought my mom yellow roses and that they were one of her favorite flowers.

I knew it was the perfect flower to fill in the gaps. After my sisters and I were done, I gathered my children and made the trip back to Tennessee to sit for my driver's test. On the way home, I was ticketed for speeding, which went in one ear and out the other, as my mom would always say.

My focus on anything outside of my mom had vanished, and the ticket plus my failed driver's test that next morning was clarity of where my focus was. Even as a Christian, I still was struggling with the question of where my mom was. Of course, she had passed, but that didn't stop me from sitting up in bed all night in the dark, asking her to visit me just once more. I needed peace. I needed my mom, but the room remained dark.

I was given a deadline on the obituary. It had to be turned in by 12:00 noon to allow time for printing. So whoever had supplied their photo, I made sure they were present, and whoever didn't was the least of my worries now. My mom's children had agreed that pink, cream, and gold would be the colors for our wardrobe. And although pink had been my favorite color, I was starting to feel like fuck pink. In my opinion, pink had represented struggle. For the many survivors, this color had still told a story of hair loss, distortion, mastectomies, millions of deaths and was rubbing me so wrong; it had started to break the skin.

My older three kids had gone out to purchase something to wear to my mom's funeral while I was working to beat my deadline on top of being sleep-deprived. I still had to purchase something for me and Gabriel to wear once I was done. I honestly wasn't in the mood to shop, but I had no choice.

As soon as I hit send, me and Gabriel went to the closest clothing store possible. I found Gabriel a dress and shoes in fifteen minutes flat. The problem came when it was time to find something that was suitable for myself.

I had looked through several racks several times, and there wasn't a pink, cream, or gold dress in sight. I had given up and started to head for the door; just as my feet were about to make that fifth step forward, I got the urge to go back. As I moved the clothes one by one, I stumbled upon a cream dress in my size that had seemed to be there just for me.

Finding that dress was like so many times before when my mom had watched over me. It seemed as if she was still right there. Fabulous had called that night and expressed how he wanted to be there to support me and the kids and although I wanted to refuse, I wasn't so sure if I was strong enough to support my kids and myself.

The next day was reserved for viewing my mom's body, so I headed back to Montgomery to walk in with my siblings. I took one look at my mom and said, "You are ready," but seeing her ready took my breath away. I was certain that a fraction of my life had to have followed my mom to her new existence, and whatever fraction of my life that was left was on borrowed time.

CHAPTER
18

It was hard to get off Kizzy's sofa, knowing that my destination was to follow behind my mom's lifeless body in a hearse, but I knew what had to be done. I thought back to my mom when she had to bury her mom and how hard it was for her. Here it was my turn to mentally fill the shoes she once wore, and they were painfully tight.

The kids got dressed at Kizzy's house, and I decided to get dressed at my mom's due to Fabulous meeting me there. The house was again full of family and friends outside and inside. They had been coming for the last two weeks to show their respect.

Once in the house, I went straight to my mom's room, and although me and several others were there getting dressed, the room felt cold and empty. After I was dressed, I headed back up front to wait for the family cars. Just as I turned around the corner, I could see Steve, my ex-husband, through the glass sliding door, talking to the kids.

Once I was outside, I could see that the pink gold and crème had come together nicely. I could hear my mom saying how awesome it was, which was her favorite line. I noticed Fabulous had arrived and was looking for a place to park, as my Aunt April was coming toward me.

"Hey, Nyla, you'll be riding with Quay and her girls."

"No problem." Fabulous walked up just as April had walked off. We hadn't talked much since the ride back from Ohio. He nodded his head to greet me, then stepped to the side. I wasn't sure where my relationship with Fabulous was heading, but at that moment, I could care less.

The pastor was ready to pray, so we all huddled up and bowed our heads as the pastor prayed. Immediately after the prayer, I looked up and asked, "Please give me strength, amen." Fabulous and I had split up since he would be driving his own car, and I was assigned a seat in the family car.

The ride with Quay and her girls was quite awkward due to us only texting and not being completely back talking. No one spoke the whole ride to the service, and to be honest, I didn't want to talk anyway. I had a window seat and looked out at the scenery as feelings of nostalgia started to kick in, thinking of all the many times I had traveled that very road with my mom.

By the time we had turned into the church parking lot, I had already been in need of a new tissue from crying so much. I could see Fabulous making his way across the parking lot to meet up with me after I was out of the car. Steve had gathered the kids, so they walked in with him. Before we could walk into the church, my mom's family was directed on what to do.

We lined up at the door, starting with Wiley, my mom's husband, her children with their spouses and children, and then her siblings two by two, resembling Noah's arch. The order was thrown completely off, with most of the family driving their own cars and the four family cars only seating four, so we didn't all arrive together. We were all given an obituary as we started moving inside the church.

The church was dark and the flowers faced out toward the family. As the music played, the line continued to move toward my mom to get the last view of her before the casket was closed forever. When it was my turn to view my mother, I remembered thinking about what I could do to erase this chapter of my life, but I came up with nothing. I bent down to kiss my mom's cheek as I had done so many times before, but this would be one that I would have to save, "I love you, Mom."

Once I was in my seat, I closed my eyes to make it–all appear like a dream that I could possibly wake from. But before I did, I glanced over at Kizzy and Quay. They were attempting to hold each other together, but I think we all lost it when they closed my mom's casket. It was over.

My mother, the woman who bled and felt pain pushing me out into the world from her body. The woman who raised me was no more. Just the thought of moving on without my mom was enough to kill me. How was I going to move on without her?

CHAPTER

When I opened my eyes, my mom was still gone. Fabulous was still a heartless bastard. Not sure why I thought he would understand but nothing about him had changed. I found myself begging for Fabulous' help far too often. Fabulous had the attitude of a husband who paid all the bills and came home to a housewife, which meant he expected to come home to a hot meal and sex. This wasn't the case. I wasn't a housewife. I worked and wanted to start a career in trucking and wherever my business degree that I had been pursuing would take me.

But lately, I was having difficulties due to my lack of focus. Although I was overly stressed, having lost my mom and trying to obtain my license, Fabulous still found a way to be a jerk. It seemed like he enjoyed the fact that my life was hell.

About two weeks after my mom's funeral, I decided maybe having sex with Fabulous would make things better between us. Maybe he was stressed due to the lack of sex. We even talked a little afterward, in which I revealed I thought sex would help us both, but it didn't. Losing my mom was taking a toll on me.

She had told me how much she desperately wanted to live. I couldn't help but wonder why God didn't honor her prayer. Over the next month, Fabulous and I grew more and more distant. We were barely speaking to each other, which seemed better than arguing. I knew it wouldn't be much longer before we had called it quits. So I started denying him. Every attempt Fabulous made for sex; each time, I just found a better way to reject him.

2020 was a rather complicated year. I found myself drinking alcohol, something I hadn't done in years to cope with Fabulous ass and the effects of the pandemic. Now that my mom was gone, my drinking became even worse. My cousin was having a birthday party and had invited me and my sisters. We had all agreed to go, but I had one more chance to obtain my license before doing so.

Fabulous had no idea I was going to test due to our lack of communication. I didn't care; all that mattered was that I walked away with my license. Early that morning, I drove up to the DMV and sprinkled holy water all over the ground. "Lord, please let me pass this test," and it was a success!

Although Fabulous and I weren't on speaking terms, I could not wait to tell him, and the kid's things were slowly trying to improve. It was Friday, so Fabulous was off early when I arrived home. He was in bed naked, not sure why since we weren't having sex.

Maybe he was sending dick pics. My overdue excitement about obtaining my CDL did little to move Fabulous. He reacted to my success like any other moment in my life, mute and not giving a damn.

In my mind, this was a jump up and down moment but I would need to wait for the kids to arrive home to have that experience. Fabulous had no family in Tennessee, only one girl he called sister and his brother who was now deceased. I had seen him show more expression for their accomplishment than I had ever seen him show for me and my children. He was never the least bit moved by anything me and my children had going on.

I had thought about backing out of the party but I had given my word. Fabulous seemed to be more excited about the party than he was with my win. Once we had gotten to Montgomery, I greeted my cousin as she pointed for Fabulous and me to come toward the alcohol.

The party gave me a feeling of guilt. How could I be partying a month after my mom was put in the ground? I took my cousin up on her offer, hoping to drink the guilt away. Fabulous, on the other hand, was taking shots and smoking weed. A characteristic about him I had rather kept secret, like so many other things I had not exposed about him.

When the party was over Fabulous kept suggesting that we go to a motel. I had been drinking, but I could most definitely drive us home. As Fabulous pulled from the driveway, the argument immediately began. Maybe going to the motel wasn't such a bad idea, but I wasn't giving Fabulous a chance to end my career by intentionally getting me pregnant.

Fabulous had told me to get the fuck out of his car at the stop sign. I called my sister to pick me up. This was the most my sister had known of Fabulous' aggressiveness, which was because – I had hidden his horrible ways from everyone all these years. To keep the monster that Fabulous really was covered up.

I pleaded with him to pick me up down the road, and he agreed. I was thankful that he no longer had a desire to go to the motel, so he proceeded to go toward I85. It took us until the next morning to make it home due to our multiple stops.

Like always, Fabulous had gathered most of his belongings and left. I was thrilled; it seemed we could wish each other well. By Monday, I was on a mission to find a job in my career, which didn't take long.

Fabulous had given me a call because, apparently, he wasn't ready to end the relationship. Any other time, it was me calling him; that was not the case this time. At this point I wasn't so sure about Fabulous' motives.

Fabulous always managed to find his way back in–the house. My period had come and I was so thankful to God because – that meant I could continue not sleeping with Fabulous, at least until we had figured out what life together or apart meant for us. That following Monday was my orientation.

Usually, right after orientation, training would start, but I was allowed to go home because I stayed so close and the company couldn't accommodate me with a trainer. While I was cleaning up the bedroom, I noticed Fabulous had purchased fucking–water. Not sure what he was lubricating as long as it wasn't me, and I didn't even bother asking him about it. Thanksgiving had come, and it was like all holidays. I cooked a huge meal, and Fabulous downed as much alcohol as he could.

After too many drinks, Fabulous was being loud and obnoxious. All I could think was why I was exposing my kids to this. I utilized one of my many antics and went to sleep late that night to avoid sleeping with Fabulous drunk ass. As soon as I was in bed, I turned my back to Fabulous and went to sleep.

The next morning, I woke up to Fabulous inside of me. I jumped up fussing, assuring him of how big of a jerk he was. When I looked back onto the bed, there was coconut oil and the fucking water I had found while cleaning up earlier in the week on the bed.

I no longer had to assume why he had purchased the fucking water. I guess it made access less disturbing. I was devastated and should've told Fabulous to leave and never come back, but I was more concerned with seeing how far he had gotten and taking a piss to hopefully prevent any chance of pregnancy. Fabulous just laid there looking pitiful almost as if his doing was justified.

Not even a week later, Fabulous did the same thing; only this time I woke up because he was gripping me and finishing up. This would be his last opportunity to violate me. He didn't even have the decency to pull out. This was it.

I demanded that Fabulous purchase a plan B, and after that, we were done. The next week, I had left for training, and I was terrified to leave my kids, which was one of the reasons why I dealt with Fabulous for so long. After about a week on the road, Fabulous had texted me to apologize for the jerk he had been and insisted that – due to his upbringing, he was basically a messed up individual.

I didn't care. I was done giving Fabulous chances. I was more serious than myocardial infarction this time. I wasn't even going to waste my time replying to him.

I was prepared for my period. I knew it was going to be hell on the road, being that – I hated public restrooms. When day one came, and my period hadn't shown up, I wasn't concerned, but after a week, I knew something was wrong.

I had to contact Fabulous, "I haven't seen my period." He replied, "We haven't even had sex." Of course, he was right; "we" hadn't had sex, although he had. A quick pregnancy test would show that Fabulous negligence was malicious.

Though I had barely gotten my foot into my career, I was already walking in the wrong direction. Negative thinking had completely taken over. "Why do I continuously allow myself to be put in these situations?

Maybe I deserve this?" I knew God had forsaken me. Every time I made one step forward, there were fifteen backward. "Why won't he just remove me from my misery?"

CHAPTER

I was convinced that God hated me. This was the first Christmas without my mother, and I was dealing with this pregnant shit. Here, I was closer to forty than thirty and pregnant with my fifth child. I was more nervous about having this baby than I was when I had my first.

After some crying, alcohol, and a tight fetal position, I knew abortion would be the only way to solve my problem. The more time I had to think, it was all clear that Fabulous had done this to me on purpose. His evil, malicious ass. My career was starting, and he wouldn't be starting his for another two years, which meant; he needed to trap a bitch a little longer.

There had been many off and ons during the course of Fabulous' and my disturbing relationship. Still, it wasn't until my career looked promising that he started sleeping with Snow White, being careful not to touch her lips, at least the ones that were attached to her face. Although I didn't want to speak to the coochie crook, I wouldn't dare let him get away with this.

Calling Fabulous made me sick to my stomach. I was sure it wasn't morning sickness but the thought of having to communicate with him alone. This was honestly the first breakup between Fabulous and me where I had really been, without a shadow of a doubt, certain that I didn't want anything else to do with him. Now, here I was once again, having to deal with him. That made me question God, I mean, I was done with his sorry ass, and then this.

Hopefully, this would be quick, and we could go back to living our separate lives. I had finished my training just in time for Christmas, so when I spoke to Fabulous, he was in Ohio for the holiday, which meant he was back to his old ways. God knows I had been up and down on whether or not to terminate the pregnancy, and at that moment, it dawned on me that I wasn't able to go through with it. Of course, I didn't want to be a single mother with a newborn again, even though it seemed I was the perfect candidate.

Yes, technically, Fabulous had raped me; at this point, reality set in as to who would want me. Me being a brown brown girl and a mother of five, with now four baby fathers. No matter what the reason was, it wasn't appealing.

I assumed if I tried making it work with Fabulous, I could be with one of my children's fathers, even if he was a poor example. Yes, he's a drunk who never made me feel safe, but at least I wouldn't be overwhelmed with the shame that came with my life. Fabulous and I had arranged to meet once he was back from his trip. The more and more I was left to think about my dilemma, the more I began to hate myself for not acting like Jordan Peele and getting out of that toxic shit.

"Who is it?" "Fab," not sure if my heart was beating overtime due to the baby or the visitor but it had indeed felt as though it would beat me to the door. "Hey, hello." Although I wanted to bust that nigga in the face for what he had done to me. I couldn't bring myself to realize what it would accomplish.

Gabriel was my one child that I worried about. She had never experienced a father figure, which devastated me because I held myself responsible. What's the chance of a woman picking the wrong man four times? No less than a man picking the wrong woman doubled that and yet the woman was still frowned upon.

Society had always praised men even though statistics had shown once a relationship was over, the man would be out faster than ShaCarri Richards, although no bodies followed. I so desperately wanted to create a two-parent home for Gabriel. Even if that meant giving up my happiness for hers.

Fabulous and I proceeded to walk to the bedroom, and only because I wasn't ready to inform the kids of my stupidity. Once in the room, Fabulous delivered the sad puppy face that he always displaced, giving off the impression that he was guilty but had no recollection of how. He would come bearing gifts, but not ones that would get a surprise reaction, a smile, or even a smirk, only a trip to the toilet. In seconds, these sticks would reveal that there was indeed life growing inside of me.

After about thirty minutes of silence, Fabulous fell back onto the bed, placing his hands on his head in disbelief. I wondered why he appeared in this state when he had been in control of the entire situation. Even though this rape wasn't brutal, it didn't hesitate to break my soul.

"What's the plan?" I found it strange that he now wanted to give me an option. I replied, "I'm not sure." Silence filled the room once again, and Fabulous turned the lights off as I curled up into the fetal position. I expected that Fabulous would leave; instead, he pulled me to the edge of the bed and began licking my toes. This was new for him and an action I would much rather not have been a participant of.

Fabulous continued working his way up his frenum needed to be cut to allow his tongue more wiggle room. Usually, when he performed oral sex on me, I laid there hoping that he would get tired before I did. Tonight was no different, and although he was great at caressing my breast, the pussy eating still hadn't improved.

I moaned, and just as he moved his extremely short tongue faster, I became louder, giving him the impression that he had succeeded. Fabulous' penis was long, and once he was done wasting time like usual, he made up for it in this area. The thought of his penis entering me when we were on good terms and, of course while I was awake, always soaked the bed.

Fabulous stroked his penis twice and slid into me, and even though I hated him, I allowed him to have his way. I can't lie; he was fucking me like he missed my pussy. The moaning may have been false before, but these were all real. It must have been true what they say about pregnancy pussy, because – Fabulous was louder than I was.

We must have gone for hours. When we were finished, we fell onto the bed, sweating with heavy breathing resembling Seabiscuit after one of his triumphs. I wish I could have dozed off to sleep, but I was no fool, at least when it came down to a cheater.

Fabulous had just sucked my toes, and in five years, he had never done that, which meant he had performed this on someone else. "How dumb could I be?" I was at a loss for words, but knowing how stupid I had been for laying down with my rapist had made me question myself. Why should I even exist, and why haven't I gotten it over with already?

CHAPTER 21

Things seemed to be coming along for me and Fabulous, even though I could barely look at myself in the mirror. I was a victim of Stockholm syndrome and I knew it was bad. I couldn't let down my kids again by running off the only man who would accept my situation even if it did feel more beneficial for him. Besides, my family was fulfilled by thinking this pregnancy could be a sign from my mom, although I knew differently.

Fabulous knew I wouldn't be going anywhere now, at least no time soon. An argument between Fabulous and I could appear out of the blue. Fabulous, and I attended my Brother PJ's party, and he was locking eyes with one of the females there all night. I suggested that we leave, though it seemed Fabulous wasn't quite ready.

After getting into the car, it appeared
Fabulous drinks had kicked in and he was on
one thousand. He was getting worse. I felt afraid
and alone, and honestly, I didn't want to take
him around my kids. I felt I had to get out of
that car because he was in no position to drive.

Somehow, we made it home. Not sure
why Fabulous thought I was going for my gun,
but he slammed me to the bed, grabbed the gun,
and went for the door. I managed to pull myself
together enough to call the police.

As always, I covered for Fabulous and
didn't tell the police he had hurt me, just that
I needed the gun back to put it in a safe place.
Fabulous had thrown my gun onto the church
parking lot up the street. The police officer took
him there to go and retrieve it.

The police handed the gun back over to
me, but not before disclosing how big of a jerk
he thought Fabulous was. Just then, It dawned
on me that I hadn't felt the baby move since a
little before Fabulous slammed me to the bed.
Although the police didn't slap a drunk and
disorderly ticket on his ass, Fabulous hadn't
sobered up.

I still needed him to drive me to the ER. As bad as I wanted to hide what was taking place from the kids, they were aware of what was going on, and they pleaded with me not to get in the car with him. It was at that moment that I realized how much I had grown to care about this baby and just hoped the baby would be okay.

At the hospital, a nurse got me to the back as fast as possible and hooked me up to some monitors. "Thank God, my baby's heart is beating." Overall, my baby was okay, as far as we could tell.

I was discharged from the Emergency Room, and Fabulous still laid there, drunk and asleep, in the chair beside the bed while I walked toward the car. I had allowed myself to get in too deep, and there was nothing I could do. Fabulous had only been verbally abusive if you didn't count the rape; now, it had become more physical.

Later, an account became available with the company I applied to for work, which meant in order to take it, I would need to be trained on the route. Matt would be the trainer assigned to me, and we were scheduled to leave at 5:00 am every morning until I was ready to operate on my own. Matt was a pretty cool dude.

He didn't make me do too much, and even though I told him the first day I had no interest in the account, he still insisted that I ride along and receive what seemed to be free money. We had hit it off like we had known each other for years. Maybe because – he made me feel safe, unlike Fabulous ass.

Matt and I talked quite often about our significant others and laughed at each other's jokes. He asked me, "You like driving?" "Well, if I don't, it's a little too late for that now, huh?" Why couldn't I have been with a guy like Matt? But Fabulous had come in and stolen my heart once again, at least that's what I was telling myself.

Matt made the time pass, and I hardly even had time to think of Fabulous and the mess that I had allowed him to make. The route usually consisted of three to four stops. We were expected to unload a portion of the cargo at each stop until the truck was empty at the final stop.

One morning, Matt and I were scheduled to pick up a load, which would start up in Georgia, and my day had already been hell due to the morning sickness I was experiencing. Not sure if I was blinded by the fact that I was pregnant, which meant morning sickness should be normal. But I should have known this would be one of those rainy days that I forgot to pack an umbrella.

Matt and I jumped into the truck and he asked, "Any music in particular you want to listen to?" I responded, "No, you can choose." Matt started the engine and gave the air pressure enough time to build, then, he proceeded to slowly drive the truck toward the gate.

The drive was rather quiet, I assumed, because – I was a bit under the weather and didn't care to talk. "What was that?" I asked as I heard a pop sound. Matt looked at me, puzzled, and said, "What?"

I replied, "You didn't hear that pop?" I was more than sure that I had heard a pop, but Matt continued to drive. About five miles later, we could feel something going on. And once I looked into the mirror, I was able to assure Matt without a doubt that one of our tires had blown out.

Matt proceeded to reach a safe haven which landed us into a patch of grass in the center of eastbound traffic. Matt jumped out to look at the damage. From the truck passenger seat, I asked, "How bad is it?"

He responded quickly, "Not too bad," in his calmly reassuring voice. Matt went for the tablet and initiated a maintenance request for a rear tandem passenger-side repair. The flat tire would put us back a couple of hours depending on how long it took the mechanic to show up to complete the job. Matt and I made small talk while we waited. Just as we were laughing about a comment I had made, I could see the mechanic pull up.

"Help is here," I said as I broke up our chain of laughs and happy conversation. He smiled and said, "Finally, I'll try to speed him along." I was happy Matt dismissed himself because – I not only needed to pee, but I needed to throw up, too.

As soon as Matt was out, I grabbed the large cup from the door and moved to the sleeper to relieve myself. Before I could finish wiping, I felt myself about to throw up. I was able to dump the cup out the window in just enough time to use it again. "I feel like shit," but before I had a chance to completely throw myself a pity party, I received a notification from Fab.

Fabulous had sent me a text telling me to be safe due to the rain that was in the forecast, followed by I love you, babe. I never believed him when he said he loved me. And I often wondered how I was going to spend the rest of my life with this man if I didn't even believe he loved me.

The tire only pushed us back an hour. It was the fastest breakdown recovery I had ever witnessed. Matt hopped back aboard and gave the throttle extra force attempting to get back the time we had lost.

We arrived at the first stop in an hour, and Matt asked if I wanted to stay in the truck. I quickly replied, "Yes." After about thirty minutes, I went into the store and purchased some chips for me and a juice for Matt. That was the least I could do for his beyond-kind gesture.

It usually took two hours per stop, which would have probably been cut down by forty-five minutes had I been pulling my weight. After about our second stop, I had discovered that my debit card had just been locked for an unauthorized transaction in Vegas. That made me ponder the situation, until my bank called and explained they needed enough time to investigate.

Rather than dwell on the raindrops that had begun saturating my body, I chose to be optimistic and take a nap in an attempt to refocus my mindset. Once I woke, Matt was backing up the truck to the dock to unload the last of the cargo before we could head back to our cars and call it a week. Matt was off every weekend, which meant so was I–at least until the gig was up and the dispatcher realized I had no intention of lifting one box.

So, lifting thousands of boxes was completely out of the universe (out of the question, so to speak) if I had to describe it. Fabulous had been extra pleasant in kicking off the neediness, which I would be adhering to for three to five business days until I got my new debit card in the mail. I texted Fab to see if it would be possible to bring me some food later.

Fabulous agreed to supply my needs, followed by what would you prefer? This I may add, was even more suspicious. After wrapping up texting with Fabulous, my under-the-weather had begun to feel like climate change, and it was hell on earth.

"Are you okay?" Matt asked me kindly, "I will be. I just need to get home," I replied. He looked at me and said, "You are not pregnant, are you? I sure hope not."

I had not told my job or any of my co-workers the news, and with the help of big clothes, I could easily hide it. When we arrived back at the terminal, I could barely get out of the truck. Matt was more than a gentleman and helped me to my car. He told me, "Feel better," before I thanked him and drove home.

Once I was in my car, I momentarily thought again, "How would it have been if I had met Matt before Fabulous, and what if he was single now?" But this man is happily married, I said to myself as I snapped out of the daze I was in. I called Fabulous to let him know I was en route to the house, and it would be appreciated if he was, too.

However, after five calls, his phone continued to go to voicemail. Fridays were usually fend for yourself at my house, which was followed by soup kitchen Saturday. It was a setup for savory Sundays, so once I was settled in, I made my rounds, confirming that the kids had indeed fended for themselves. I just knew Fab would have rang the doorbell or called by now, but a quick glance at my phone revealed that this was not the case.

I began to call and text Fabulous repeatedly, and after about sixty times of hearing his sorry-ass voice on his outgoing voicemail, I decided to call it a night. About 6:00 a.m. the next morning, Fabulous sent me a text in which he disclosed Alabama had just beaten Ohio in the Southeastern Conference. All I could think about was the defense he was going to need for the round two that would be following.

I called that bastard immediately after the text. He continued to say he was asleep, and this was no lie. I wasn't willing to accept the excuse, which drove Fabulous to confess that he had been out with a bitch.

Now – I knew why the previous day had reminded me of the many times I had been unprepared for the weather. Screaming to the top of my lungs was getting nowhere because—it appeared I was talking to myself. At one point, I think his punk ass had even fallen asleep. Fabulous came over the next day, I guess, with hopes of giving me time to cool off.

Still, all I wanted to do was hit his bitch-ass in his face, but even more–so, I wanted details. Not sure what I thought would come of this, but I wanted to know did you do anal? Did you eat her pussy? Did you kiss her, and he revealed it all, even showing me her picture, which was the nail in the coffin.

To make matters worse, she was light-skinned and–again, like so many times before, when I felt like I had underbid and the auction had gone in favor of the opponent. At this point, I couldn't help but think that no matter how much of a nympho or submissive I was willing to be, my brown brown skin was no match for the lighter skin. Early that week, Steve had come across my Facebook archive, and the man that I once thought couldn't get enough of brown brown skin had chosen to now be represented by a light-skinned female as well.

Men never looked at us as beautiful, but only as being aggressive, combative, and good for fucking was becoming a reality to me. The only thing left to do was establish an exit plan that would end my hurt permanently since my skin wasn't getting any lighter. This meant there was only one way to do this.

CHAPTER

There was only one month left until I gave birth to a baby boy and before my crummy life would end. Fabulous had three daughters already, and this new arrival would be his first son. He tried to give off the impression he was thrilled to those who had no clue of the manipulative narcissist he was behind closed doors.

Fabulous had not been to one doctor visit or ultrasound viewing; he was back to being a selfish bitch. I was sure to make all my prenatal visits on the grounds of my baby being innocent. There was no way I was allowing him to be hurt behind mine and Fabulous' bullshit.

Jokingly – I would get asked why I chose to start over, being that – I had adult children. My answer was always the same, "I didn't choose this." I was completely over Fabulous' shit.

I anticipated having this baby so I could follow through with my exit plan. It wasn't just Fabulous. I was over my life, too – period. Always being the darkest in the room was attached to condescending behavior from the lights and whites. And thanks to the work of The Master, we Brown Browns didn't matter, so no one ever felt ashamed by their behavior, just entitled.

I just couldn't take it anymore. I was tired of being pushed over and looked over for something which I had no control over. I mean, I didn't get a menu to choose my skin color because – I sure wouldn't have wanted brown brown skin.

At this juncture, I hated my skin and what was within me. I had just about purchased everything the baby would need. Fabulous had made a couple of purchases, but anytime he did, he would only deduct it from his portion of the mortgage money.

Fabulous was at my house full time now, which meant every day was worse than the day before. He was still nasty and insisted on leaving a mess for me and the kids to clean. What is it going to be like with a new baby?

I had no final conclusion of what was going to happen to my children after I was gone. However; I was exhausted, and my clock-out time was near. I was already battling depression with no gloves, and this was the only pregnancy that I remembered being painful just when the baby would move. I was beyond miserable.

Lorenzo Jr. had a birthday coming up, and he had made it clear that he didn't want to share his birthday with a baby or he would be leaving. I did as much in my power to honor Lorenzo Jr.'s wishes. Not that if the baby came, I could do much to stop him. Lately, me and Lorenzo Jr. hadn't been seeing eye to eye. And the only reason I even considered not taking a laxative to push this pregnancy along was due to the feelings of the kids as a whole.

The kids weren't elated by the news of their newest sibling, which I acknowledged due to the fact they were all older and enjoying their lives. They knew I could be in need of a babysitter soon. Lorenzo Jr. was just doing too much, though.

He had always been that one child that I had to stay on. So, if presented with the challenge, I had always made myself willing and available. Since he had turned eighteen, it was more like a vendetta, and his vendetta-like behavior had his paternal grandparents' names written all over it.

Over the years, my older kids' grandparents had done so much to try and destroy me, like I wasn't all they had left. Lorenzo's mom had even tried to have my kids taken away from me, claiming abuse and neglect. This bitch had no regret nor shame for what may have happened to my other kids as long as she could hurt me.

No matter how much Lorenzo Jr. knew or saw coming up, he still decided to side with his evil grandparents. He engaged in conversation that discredited my character. Much like Fabulous had been, Lorenzo Jr. encouraged any shenanigans that made me look like shit.

Lorenzo's mom wanted him to be with a white girl or someone much lighter than me. She had subliminally conveyed the message to her other two sons, and now, she began indoctrinating into Lorenzo Jr's mind. Colorism, betrayal, and disappointment were normal for me.

The fact that – my son still found a reason to hate me, just killed me. Although I had always been present for him and the countless sacrifices I had made over the years on his behalf, only seemed to validate that — I would never be up to standard. I wasn't sure why God was choosing to allow my feelings to be hurt time after time by people I had loved and trusted.

This was one of the many reasons which resulted in my soul being shattered. I had enough to deal with, but it always seemed my plate was never full enough. I was starting to question if God had my plate mixed up with someone else's and had severed me their portion.

I had done everything for my kids. I expected the disloyalty from Fabulous, but never my kids, who had been there since day one to witness my many struggles to keep the lights on and food on the table. After doing all I could to honor Lorenzo's wishes, the very next day, I was in the pharmacy buying castor oil. I was hoping to speed along my labor and nothing was happening.

This would be the fourth time I had performed this method during a pregnancy, and the first time it didn't work. My method was turning into a disaster. The only thing that was happening was vomiting and diarrhea. Over the next week, I was feeling weak, like nothing I had ever experienced in my other pregnancies. It had even become hard for me to get out of bed.

When I went in for my weekly check-up, I begged the Doctor to induce my labor, and she agreed that the following weekend would be best. Once I was home, I did my best to gather my bags and prepare myself to be a mother for the fifth time. I hadn't told Fabulous that I would be giving birth the next day, and neither did I intend to. I didn't need him over me, pretending to care when he was the reason for this Vale of tears.

Fabulous was due to go in for work the next morning. The scheme was to be gone and delivered before he could catch wind of what was happening. Later that night, I was startled by my phone.

"Hello, it's Lisa over at labor and delivery. I just wanted to inform you that we are going to need to reschedule you–" At that point, I began to cry uncontrollably. Unfortunately, Fabulous overheard the conversation and demanded that he be in the room. How bad must our relationship have been that all I could think was that his only motive for even wanting to be present was to watch me in pain?

I was so over it all; nothing mattered anymore. I couldn't care less at that point if he was present or not. I knew my time was short, and fussing with him only stressed me out more.

I still didn't know of anyone that could fill my shoes or that was going to be a better mother to my kids than me once I was gone. But what I did know was that I had checked out a long time ago. My body was the only thing left on this earth and it needed to join my soul wherever it resided.

CHAPTER 23

It was Sunday morning. I was startled by my phone once again. Only this time, the caller sounded charismatic, which was an exchange for my aspiration.

It was Lisa, the nurse from labor and delivery, informing me that they were ready for me. Fabulous grabbed the suitcases that I had prepared for the baby and me and put them in the car while I proceeded to get dressed. Still feeling under the weather was an understatement when it came down to how I felt, and I had no fucking clue why.

Moving with a sense of urgency was out of the question. Hell, I could barely lift a leg although I was eager to give birth. After I removed my clothes, I gave my stretched marked covered stomach one last look and immediately began to cry.

I didn't want to become a mom for the fifth time, even though I knew it was happening one way or another. If only I had left Fabulous before his desperation kicked in. Just maybe, I could have gotten past enough of the hurt, and I wouldn't be counting my days.

Of course, I couldn't blame Fabulous for all my hurt no more than I could blame the others who had damaged me. It took them all. If I must take accountability, it was also me that got me in this shit.

"Are you ready?" He yelled to me from the other room, and I responded, "No, give me a second." Fabulous had to have heard me crying, yet he never asked if I was okay or why. Fabulous had been insisting all week that my not feeling well was all in my head, which was just another level of his selfishness.

I threw on the maxi dress the best way that I could, slid on my flip-flops, and tucked my ID and debit card into my bra. I said a prayer even though I was down to half a mustard seed of faith. I then headed toward the front of the house.

Chapter 23

When I reached the front, I gathered up the kids with tears still in my eyes. With a lack of enthusiasm, I announced that it was time. The older kids said little to ease my situation. Grabiel, my youngest, on the other hand, expressed an abundance of exhilaration for the new edition to the already shattering family. Even though the older kids were disappointed and probably a bit disgusted, they still hugged me and said that they loved me. This only hurt me more because – I was no longer strong enough to fight for my happiness or my life.

The ride to the hospital was quiet. I could see Fabulous looking at me from my peripheral vision, but I still continued to look straight ahead. Fabulous stopped the car in front of the hospital's automatic doors labeled emergency. I am sure to get me closer to the building due to my speed now being that of a snail and not because he cared. Before I could comfortably place my derriere in the chair, Fabulous walked through the double doors with an Oscar-winning performance portraying the concerned boyfriend and father-to-be.

"Where do you have to go?" "Labor and delivery?" The walk through the hospital was rather rough. Even passing by the pictures of happy families with their new baby, intended to persuade the terrified mother-to-be to remain calm and happy, didn't convince me.

As Fabulous continued to move toward the corridor, that broke off, exposing one room that would be designated for me to deliver my son in. He exemplified unsympathetic behavior by not even caring enough for me to get me a fucking wheelchair. After what felt like the Million Man March, I finally made it to the check-in desk runner up to Fabulous panting like a horse in triple-digit heat with no water.

"What's your name, ma'am," the receptionist asked, "Nyla Cox." After a quick search, she replied, "Right this way." The nurse pulled up a wheelchair and invited me to take a seat.

I'm sure this wasn't new for her but the hospitality she provided at that moment for me was beyond appreciated. My whole body felt like it was that of a vase, and a terrible two-year-old was seconds away from pushing me off the shelf. Seeing it up close, the room selected for me wasn't that attractive, even though it was just for delivering. It was giving off bad energy, along with the lassie next door screaming like she had just reached the top of Mount Everest.

The nurse handed me a gown and gave me instructions that included my butt hanging out, which didn't bother me. My visit was destined for much more exposure, and I wanted this baby out! After I had followed the nurse's orders, she returned to the room with the longest cue tip I had ever seen, requesting to shove it into my nose to perform a COVID test.

It would take a total of five tries to successfully complete the test; which resulted in the nurse being my newest enemy. When the nurse was done, she entered a VHS tape into a tape player that displayed a video meant to educate me on the epidural. It was at that very moment that I learned that the VHS tape and tape player wasn't obsolete!

The nurse would leave the room only to return with every personal protective equipment known to man to reveal to me that my COVID test was indeed positive. This would have been the perfect time for Fabulous to extend an apology for insisting nothing was wrong with me. Instead, he continued playing on his phone, showing his lack of interest in my care.

Hours in, my contractions were becoming stronger. I had already declined an epidural but not opioids, so at this point, something had to give. With Gabriel, my fourth child, I had a fear of the epidural, and although I was ready to die, I didn't want it to be like this. With this baby to come, it was no different, so I agreed to have opioids administered through my IV. I could rest in between contractions, although the resting period was very short.

After about nine hours of contractions, the doctor entered the room to check my cervix and determined that I was indeed ready to push. The doctor instructed me to place my heels into the stirrups, slide my bottom to the edge of the bed and, wait for the next contraction, then push. "I see the head, and there is lots of hair. Big push here! Again!"

After five pushes, he was out. Tears began to roll down my face and I was unsure if they were tears of joy or heartbreak. Then the doctor laid the crying unwashed baby onto my chest. Looking into the baby's eyes, I knew he needed me but I also knew I didn't have anything to give; so as the baby continued to cry so did I.

Maybe it was selfish of me to leave my children behind, one being my new baby and all. But I didn't have the strength to move on. And so – I was still moving forward with my plan one way or another.

Chapter 23

CHAPTER 24

"Dark-skinned women are ugly. They don't come close to the beauty of a light or white chick. They're aggressive and, of course, were a good fuck but nothing more. One would never marry us and treat us how any woman deserved to be treated. If one did truly love us, they'd never take us seriously enough to love us til death do us part."

Pulling myself together this morning wasn't happening. My thoughts had completely taken over; my body was just accompanying the actions that resulted from these thoughts. I had managed to live a bit longer than I had initially predicted.

I was in love with my new baby boy. Heck, all of my kids, but on top of my current depression about my already troubled life, a new unsettling postpartum depression emerged. With my other kids, I experienced similar symptoms, but never to this degree. Most days, I was sad to be happy, and on other days I was happy to be sad; and this morning was one of those mornings.

I was uneducated on Postpartum depression; it seemed that anyone I knew had no real knowledge of the condition either. Being with my baby gave me a sense of joy, but whenever I breastfed him, that kicked my depression up a notch. While feeding him, I could only think of what I didn't have, what I would never have, and why I had been put in this position to not have.

Here I was at thirty-eight years old in an unfaithful unmarried relationship, with a man I no longer adored, five kids, one being a newborn, four baby fathers and dark skinned. I was aware of my part in this shit. I was convinced that all my problems were fueled by the color of my skin though. I mean – here it was 2024, and darker women were still wearing lighter makeup to appear lighter and even going through procedures to lighten their skin pigmentation.

I wasn't the only brown brown skin woman in the world. I was sure so many of us had been victims of society treating us like we were less. Apparently, no matter how much I loved my kids it had become clear to me that taking my own life would not only make them well-off, it would give them the opportunities that I didn't have.

I knew if my kids had the money which they stand to gain once I was gone. At least their skin color wouldn't hinder them, and they could buy happiness if they needed to. The missed opportunities, being belittled, and the jokes people said was a treatment that had been very real and damaging for me trailing back as far as I could remember. Even during slavery, my dark skin would have landed dead last in a category of two. I mean how many celebrities only marry and father their kids with light or white women?

Laying there, I knew that I wouldn't be making it another twenty-four hours. Life was still having its way with me. Things were only getting worse for Fabulous and I. He didn't even help me with the baby.

On top of things, he had completed his HVAC technician program, so he was making more money. Fabulous had no use for me at this point. He had reached his goal, so I knew it was only a matter of time before he didn't come home or picked a fight in which he would choose to leave for good.

After removing my baby from my breast, I knew I had to move quickly if my plan was going to work. I gathered all my insurance documents and any necessary forms that Emerald would need to collect on my life insurance policy, and laid them on her bed in plain sight for her, out of sight of Fabulous. Tears were out of the question. I had cried half of my life; it had done me no good. Yeah, I knew my kids would be sad, but they'd eventually get over it.

Fabulous got off at one o'clock on Saturdays, and Emerald had taken her siblings out for a day of fun to give me a break. So – it would be Fabulous who would come in to find me deceased. I hated that my baby would be laying next to me when I took my last breath, but I was certain that this had to happen, and there was no going back. The bottle of sleeping pills and water that I selected as my choice for the kill sat on the nightstand.

It was February 24, 2024; it seemed that all was perfect. My phone didn't ring; although, my siblings had been trying to reach me for months. It was quiet. I then looked over at my baby sleeping peacefully as he was moments

away from loosing his mother; I began to write
my suicide note.

To my Kids,

(Please destroy this letter once you have read it.)

I love you all beyond measure, and I'm sorry
that I wasn't strong enough to continue on with my
life. Unfortunately, as you all know, there's no secret
to dark skin not being favored by society. I am tired.
On top of living amongst brainwashed individuals
that feed the narrative that encourages colorism, I've in
return made many mistakes to try and make up for it,
which resulted in failures.

I think all five of you are beautiful but the
choice that I am making now is one that I feel will
benefit you all and set you up for life. So that no matter
if you have brown or brown brown skin, you will never
have to settle for less.

Love, Mom

On my check ups, I was sure to inform my doctors and document how my depression was winning. Just like so many other women's cries had gone unheard, so did mine. When it all boiled then simmered, let's just say I was leaving it up to the insurance company and the doctor's office to fight it out in court. I had done my research, and I know the doctors had failed to protect me from myself.

It was 11:30 am, which gave me just enough time to complete my mission and the baby wouldn't be left alone for too long. I gave my son one final kiss and whispered into his ear that I loved him. I began placing the pills into my mouth three at a time, and then I took a sip of water.

Pills that I once had to help me sleep due to my depression, would now be helping me to fall asleep for good. The number twenty-four seemed to be no coincidence because – after I consumed the 24th pill, my body began to feel heavy. I fell back onto the pillow. I could see my baby out of the corner of my eye. I remember thinking what if this was the day Fabulous decided not to come home?

Just as I began to have regret, I wanted to run to the toilet to place my hand down my throat to regurgitate, but my legs wouldn't move. My breathing had become very heavy as I attempted to throw my hands up to place my fingers in my mouth. Although my arms wouldn't move, they felt as if they were pinned to the bed.

I guess I wasn't cried-out because – tears began to roll down my face as my breathing became even heavier. I knew there was nothing I could do to reverse what had been done. I thought of my kids just as my eyes closed, and then, there was nothing.

Beyond Skin

How dare our skin be the ultimate factor for
what determines importance.

How dare we be so selfishly blind that we'd rather practice reluctance.

What's the harm in getting to know the beauty
which lies within,

Instead of allowing assumption and ignorance to
delay one's win?

There's so much more which can be used to de-
fine a person.

Like their brain, their smile, loyalty – things
which are more certain.

It appears that the plan for destruction has pre-
vailed. Although our ancestors were enslaved
and whipped to prevent that epic fail.

Moving forward, we must learn to love one another ..

In lieu of making predictions off what's revealed
by the cover.

Many of us have experienced racism and colorism at least once in our lifetime. For women, these hardships can be far more detrimental, leading up to cries for help that often go unheard. It is at those moments that she must reach deep within to expose the woman her Creator has shaped her to be. How much effort does it really take to give up?

No matter how extremely bad your circumstances are, know that you are a conqueror. The woman who demands love, peace, and respect lies dormant in us all until summoned. So, whenever feelings of depression, regret, or suicide are rising up, gear up and fight because – you were not created to be defeated. It's showtime! No matter how strong women are, we sometimes allow our feelings to affect our emotions, which can test our sanity, but that is why we have serenity. Being born black and rejected cannot be controlled, although allowing yourself to just never be enough can.

If you or someone you know is thinking about suicide and seeking emotional support, there are crisis lines available via phone, chat, or text. National Suicide Prevention Lifeline 1-800-273-TALK(8255).

SCAN ME

Call or Text:
770-240-0089 Press Extension 1
Web: KLEpub.com
Email Services@klepub.com

It's time to start and finish   **YOUR Story!**

KLE Publishing specializes in helping people become authors. In as little as 15 to 90 days, we can help you develop your books and e-books and publish to 39,000 outlets! We also offer audiobook services.

Write, Edit, Format, Publish
We can help from
Start to Finish.